DCI Chrissie Charles
Book two

HEARTLESS

PAMELA GRIFFITHS

Pamela Griffiths

DCI Chrissie Charles

Book two

Heartless

This novel is entirely a work of fiction, the names, characters
and incidents portrayed in it are the work of the author's
imagination. Any resemblance to actual persons, living or dead,
is entirely coincidental.

Great Britain

First published 2017

Classification - Fiction

Crime Thriller

ISBN: 10: 1253683899
ISBN-13: 9781523683895

Reviews and praise

'The Stamp Master'
(Book one)
DCI Chrissie Charles detective thriller novels.

'Read this book in 6hrs could not put it down had me gripped, what a brilliant read, my husband and children had to get their own evening meal.'

'I have just finished reading The Stamp Master novel and it was absolutely brilliant and that's the truth, because I don't read books because I lose concentration easily. It kept me on the edge of my seat. Pamela Griffiths is one hell of a good writer. Please try it out you won't be disappointed. The Stamp Master by Pamela Griffiths.'

'I am enjoying the story and greatly admire you for actually finishing the book and getting it published. I am still writing and editing my novels. I look forward to reading the next one and seeing your writing style develop
Good luck.'

'Just finished reading The Stamp Master by Pamela Griffiths What a fab read. Read it in less than 48 hours, could not put it down.'

'It was one of the best books I've read. Had me hooked from the first page.'

Reviews for 'The Stamp Master' on amazon.co.uk.

5.0 out of 5 stars
Give it a go!
On 28 Jun. 2014
'I read this book in one sitting. If you enjoy books that keep you guessing to the end this is the book for you, I couldn't put it down until all was revealed. I will be looking forward to reading more novels from this author.'

5.0 out of 5 stars
Excellent!!
On 30 May 2014
Format: Kindle Edition
'Highly recommended serial killer thriller. Really enjoyed it! Can't wait for the next instalment! A good read.'

5.0 out of 5 stars
'Really enjoyed this hope there will be another one to follow...'

On 20 July 2014
Format: Kindle Edition Verified Purchase
'Really enjoyed this hope there will be another one to follow just couldn't put it down.
Keep up the good work.'

5.0 out of 5 stars
'Wow.'

The thing about smart people is that
They sound crazy to dumb people

Einstein

For my family and friends, thank you all for your
continued support and encouragement.

A big thank you to all the people who purchase
and read my books, without whom I wouldn't be
writing at all.

ACKNOWLEDGMENTS

Thank you to my daughter Angela Shevrin for reading and reviewing Heartless before I submitted it for publication.

Thank you to my Granddaughter Shannon Griffiths for drawing the heart that I used on the front cover of Heartless. And for giving me permission to use it.

PROLOGUE:

The operating theatre was very basic to say the least. It had seen better days. There were cobwebs in the corners; flies were caught in the many webs awaiting their fate. The walls were in desperate need of a coat of paint to cover the peeling remnants of the paint that had been there from many years ago.

An emergency generator was now providing the power to light the building and the operating area. The decaying building had once been a hospital; it had been closed down many years ago. It had been abandoned and left to decay. Many of the old beds and equipment had been locked away in a warehouse next to the emergency generator room.

The time had now come to reopen this decaying operating theatre, to perform what had now become a normal occurrence for heart patients who needed a transplant.

A surgeon was scrubbed, gowned and masked, ready to perform the surgery. It was as though time had been rewound, to an era before heart transplants had even been imagined.

There was a patient on the operating table, being kept alive with a heart bypass machine. The machine was reconditioned and very old, it wasn't ideal, but it did the job. The donor was a young male, in his early twenties; he had been anaesthetized and ready to unwillingly donate his healthy heart to someone who needed it.

The donor's heart would serve its purpose in this project, in the surgeon's opinion.

The recipient was also in the operating theatre almost ready to receive the donor's heart. This operation had been performed numerous times and it was now almost commonplace.

Scrubbed up and ready for the operation was the surgeon's team. A feeling of nostalgia was overcoming the surgeon. The hospital still had many pungent smells that lingered from the past. Remnants of the buildings' former existence still remained within its walls. Trying to recreate its many tales of hope, death, saving lives, and a strict protocol.

The nurse was terrified of the surgeon. She had been kidnapped and held captive and was being used in the team of three. The team of three consisted of the surgeon, the nurse and a man who was dressed in scrubs. The nurse didn't know who the man was, she wondered if he had been kidnapped too, but he seemed to know what he was doing.

The distinctive redolence of disinfectant was like being taken back to the old days when all hospitals had this smell.

The surgeon was beginning to sweat under the large overhead light that would illuminate the operating table for the duration of intricate surgery.

The young brunette nurse mopped the sweat from the surgeon's brow as the procedure was about to take place.

'Scalpel' the surgeon held out a hand to receive it. A bead of sweat began its journey down towards the mask that covered a mouth that was hiding a smirk.

'Let there be life' the surgeon said as the scalpel sliced open the chest of the donor.

1

DCI Chrissie Charles was sitting at her desk working her way through the paperwork in front of her. She had been studying the details of a missing person report from a few months ago. Apparently a young nurse had gone missing and no one had heard or seen anything of her since then. There were also a few other cases she was working on, but nothing really serious at the moment. She was glad of the respite following the Stamp Master case last year. That had been a particularly harrowing case for all concerned.

Chrissie's phone bleeped, she had received a message from her partner Dr Janny Stowers; a consultant in cardiology and the Medical Examiner. She worked with Chrissie when she was called upon to use her expertise in forensic science.

'Hi sexy, meet me for lunch in Jack's café
luv u xxx.'

Chrissie sent a reply.

'Ok hussy pussy
luv u xxx.'

Following the horrendous stamp master case last year, the two women had grown even closer than before. They were lovers and best friends, but they didn't live together that wasn't their thing. What they had together was very special and it worked well for them both.

Chrissie had thought she was going to lose Janny when the stamp master murderer had stabbed her. Luckily Janny had pulled through.

Janny had some weird near death experience following the stabbing. As she had fought for her life on the hospital operating theatre, she felt herself floating above the scene as though she was a spectator there. She now believed that the near death experience tales she had heard about in her line of work, had some element of truth in them.

This had changed Janny; she didn't see things in the same way as she had done previously. Chrissie felt that Janny was suffering from some sort of stress related syndrome.

Janny had tried to fob off the experience too, but now she was getting some really weird things happening to her. She didn't know if it was real or just some symptom following the horrendous things that had occurred. She had kept an open mind.

The months following that fateful occurrence, had been both stressful and a relief. Janny received counselling to help her get back on track. It was hard to make any sense of what had happened. Chrissie was unbelievably relieved that Janny had survived. Janny was just glad to be alive.

Life was beginning to return to some sort of normality for them now. It would always be there in their subconscious minds forever, but they had both tried very hard to file the Stamp Master case where it belonged. It was in the archive records department, filed away forever.

*

Sally burst into Chrissie's office balancing a cup of coffee and a small plate of biscuits using an elbow and a foot to negotiate the door. Chrissie's secretary Sally was like a breath of fresh air, her bubbly personality always shone through.

'Here you go, coffee and biscuits to keep you going until lunchtime.'

'Oh thanks Sally' Chrissie said as she quickly made a space in the middle of the paperwork on her desk.

Sally precariously maneuvered the cup and biscuits into the space without spilling the contents. A trick she had mastered quickly when she had started working for Chrissie.

'Can I get you anything else?'

'No thanks Sally, this is lovely?'

Sally Williams, Chrissie's secretary, breezed out of her office like a breath of fresh air. Thirty eight year old Sally Williams had been married to her husband Richard for many years. The couple hadn't been blessed with any children. It wasn't known if it was by choice or whether it was because they were unable to conceive. Sally never let on.

She is such a treasure.' Chrissie thought as she

watched her leave.

Reading the reports on her desk whilst dunking a biscuit into her coffee wasn't a good idea. She had to try and make sure she didn't slop her coffee all over the place. Then she cursed under her breath as the end of the biscuit broke off and fell into the cup.

Her mind began to wander from the report she was reading. Her thoughts had drifted towards Janny and her weird dreams. She had been having quite a lot of them recently. Janny had the usual nightmares and flashbacks. This was caused by the post-traumatic stress she had been suffering from. But they appeared to be getting less. These new dreams were taking over. Janny had tried to explain to Chrissie, what she referred to as her special dreams. She always informed her as and when they appeared to her. It was probably nothing and just a normal reaction to the trauma she had experienced.

The phone rang Chrissie answered it.

It was Detective Sergeant Mike Hartley.

'I've just heard that a patient has escaped from the psychiatric secure unit at Lockington Royal Infirmary. The hospital security officers are out looking for her now.'

'Can you get a few of our officers out there to help, and put out a BOLO (be on the lookout for) we need to find her ASAP.'

'Will do, her name is Mary Smithe; she has been

diagnosed as being a schizophrenic. She is fifty-five years old and could be potentially dangerous if confronted.' Mike warned her.

'Ok Mike, I'll leave it up to you, get James to help out and ask him to organize a full search of the area.'

'Will do, I'll be in touch.' Mike told her.

'*Shit.*' Chrissie thought out loud.

Detective Sergeant Mike Hartley contacted Detective Inspector James Barrow; and between them they worked out how they were going to handle this. They had to move quickly, they didn't want Mary Smithe on the run for too long, anything could happen.

*

Mary Smithe was hiding from the nurses; she didn't want to go back into the hospital psychiatric unit. The voices had told her she would be safe if she could escape. She moved stealthily away from the hospital grounds keeping out of sight and trying not to draw any attention to herself. The voices had warned her not to be noticed, this was very important if she wanted to stay free.

Mary knew that she would have to eat and sleep rough from now on. The voices would have to tell her where she could go. She knew she could rely on them. This was an adventure, much better than being drugged up on some stupid hospital ward. It was full of psychiatric patients, along with stupid doctors and nurses. She didn't need to be there, she was fine as long as she had the voices to guide her. She would now be free and safe from all those evil medical staff in there.

Following the tree lined walkways, running through the backs of the surrounding buildings, Mary set off on her adventure.

'This was going to be fun.' She thought.

Luckily it was a warm dry, humid day so Mary didn't have to worry about battling the elements at least. The voices had told her she didn't have to worry about anything. Her only task at the moment was to escape without being seen. It was important to get away without leaving any tell-tale signs for the cops to follow.

*

James and Mike were in the psychiatric unit interviewing the ward manager and staff who worked there. Apparently Mary had escaped from the ward as a visitor had entered. There was a key coded lock on the main door, which had been released when a visitor was buzzed in. Mary had passed the visitor going out as the visitor entered. No one noticed Mary had gone until it was time for her meds, by that time a few hours had expired. Long enough for Mary to make a good escape.

'Mary is fine when she stays on her medication, but recently she has been missing out some of her doses. Hence her re-admission to this ward. She has been sectioned for her own safety and the safety of others.' The ward manager told them. '

'Thank you for your help, please contact us if she returns, or if you remember anything that could help us to find her.' James told him as he passed him a card with his contact number on it.

As they left the hospital James and Mike scanned the area and noticed the security officers wandering around the grounds.

'I reckon she's long gone by now.' Mike said.

'More than likely, but who knows where she could have gone? She could be anywhere by now, which makes our job a whole lot harder. Let's get a team on this now. We'll start with the wooded walkways nearby, and then we'll go from there.' James said as he called it in.

Mike called in for some ground crew to help in the search. This was a glorified missing person case, so they hoped it wouldn't take too long to locate Mary Smithe. The main problem was that they didn't know how Mary would react to hearing the voices again. She was apparently a lovely lady when on her medication, but she didn't like not being able to hear the comforting voices in her head. So quite often she would stop taking her medication. This then causes the episodes that would end up with her being sectioned again. She had spent quite a lot of time in and out of the psychiatric hospital acute wards.

Going on the information that the ward manager had told them. Mary would be ok for a while, but then she would start to show her schizophrenic tendencies again. She would then become unpredictable. When she was in this state she could be capable of anything.

Chrissie had been informed of what was happening. She sighed as she thought about what could happen if Mary Smithe wasn't found soon. She sat at her desk with her head in her hands; then she started to write another mundane report.

2

Mary hadn't taken much baggage with her when she had escaped from the hospital. She had left with a small backpack that contained a change of clothes. In the backpack was a pair of light blue jeans, a plain T-shirt in dark blue. She had a couple of changes of underwear and a couple of clean tops a light hoodie top and a lightweight raincoat. She had packed a roll on deodorant so she wouldn't smell like a vagrant, which was important. The voices had warned her of the dangers of drawing attention to herself. If she didn't keep herself clean she would start to smell, and that would attract people to notice her. She would do what the voices had told her to do. She would be safe if she listened to them.

Her backpack had also included a bottle of water, some snack food including crisps and biscuits; she had collected these from the hospital. The art was in the packing; she had managed to get all these things into a relatively small bag. Taking out a small black leather purse, she checked the money inside it. There was around one hundred pounds in it. This was money that she had saved herself, along with some cash that she had stolen from a few of the patients. It would last her for a while if she was careful not to spend it too quickly.

The voices had warned her to stay away from the beaten track, to blend into the background. She was being very cautious; she followed the dirt track in the woodland down towards a stream. Mary removed the clothes she was wearing and put on the clean jeans and T-shirt. She washed the clothes she had taken off in the running water, and then dried them in the hot sun by the side of the stream. Once her clothes had completely dried, she rolled them up carefully to prevent creasing, and put them into her backpack.

Mary was aware that she would have to move out of the area as soon as possible to stay free. The voices had told her what she should do. Without drawing any attention to herself, she made her way to the bus station and boarded a bus.

The sun was very hot, it was blaring down on all who were out in it. The bus was stifling, even though all the windows were open. Mary sat in a window seat staring out at the many people who were going about their daily business. They were all like insects doing what was expected of them.

There was no hiding from the intense heat, it was very hot.

'Not a good day for escaping from a psychiatric hospital.' Mary thought.

She set off on her continuing adventure, along with the voices, which were her trusted friends and advisors. The bus set off and Mary let out a breath of relief. This part had gone smoothly and according to plan, just like the voices told her it would.

No one had given her a second glance, she was an older woman, dressed casually, minding her own business. There was nothing at all to draw attention to her. Mary blended in nicely on the hot sticky bus. The voices talked to her throughout the journey, Mary knew she couldn't answer them, for fear of getting noticed, but she was listening carefully to what they were telling her. She knew how important it was not to get into a full-scale conversation with them. This was one of the reasons why she had been sectioned in the first place.

Mary looked out of the window; listening to the voices, they were talking to her inside her head. She was watching the world go by from her vantage point. She shut her eyes for a few moments to take in what the voices were saying to her. They were looking out for her and she felt safe now.

*

Dr Janny Stowers was looking through her office window, staring down at the melting road beneath.

'It's sod's law that we have to work while the sun is shining, it'll probably rain over the weekend when we're both off work.' She thought.

Janny looked at her mobile; there was the reply from Chrissie to her earlier message.

'Hussy Pussy? I'll give her Hussy Pussy.' Janny thought as she looked at the time.

She rang Chrissie.

'Hi darling, how's it going?' Janny asked, deciding to leave the hussy pussy comment until she saw Chrissie in person.

'Everything's ok here love; I'll fill you in over

lunch. How's your day going'?

'Not too bad, I did an open heart op earlier, and I've got an outpatient clinic this afternoon, nothing too taxing at the moment. I'm feeling a bit hungry already, I'll see you soon.'

'See you soon my love.'

Following the call, Chrissie asked Sally to get James on the phone.

'What's happening with the missing patient James, any news yet'?

'Nothing yet, we've got some constables out there scouring the countryside just in case she's hiding in the rough countryside. A couple of police dogs with their handlers are out there too. There hasn't been any sign of her yet, no one has seen hide nor hair of her. She's being very elusive at the moment.' James informed her.

'Carry on with the search for now; if we don't find her soon we'll leave it to missing persons to sort. I'm only doing this to help out for now while things are quiet here and to keep you guys gainfully employed.' Chrissie told them.

The collection of missing person reports on her desk was quite off putting; she thought she was above all this. Because her caseload was very low at the moment; she had been assigned to help out in various other departments if they needed it.

Most of the cases she had at the moment were cases that hadn't been closed or resolved, some of them dating back months. With missing persons, sometimes it was almost impossible to find them. Some of the missing people just didn't want to be found, there was a fine line as to whether or not the cases should be followed through. It was important to make sure that there was no wrong doing involved. Chrissie noticed that there had been a few cases over the last few weeks that were intriguing. A young nurse and two young men had gone missing within a week or two of each other. She made a mental note to herself to check this out.

Chrissie didn't know which was worse, having the big homicide cases or dealing with these run of the mill cases. Following the Stamp Master case, this lull was a good thing in a way. It gave her the chance to recharge her batteries. She tidied up the paperwork that was scattered all over her desk and put the reports back into their appropriate files. Chrissie then freshened up with a wet wipe and a spray of deodorant ready to meet up with Janny for lunch.

'God it's bloody hot.' She thought.

3

The dreams Janny had been experiencing following her near death state, had become more frequent. Janny couldn't help feeling that the dreams meant something. She didn't know how to interpret what they meant yet, but she knew something was happening to her, something that she couldn't explain.

'I know it sounds insane, but I am certain that the dreams are important in some way.' Janny explained.

'It could be a side effect of the stress you've been under, it might just be nature's way of getting your brain back to normal again' Chrissie told her.

'Since when did you become a shrink? I've already talked about it with my therapist and she didn't think it was anything serious. I can't help feeling it is though.'

The two women sat across from each other at the small table. They were sitting in a small recess, which made it extra private and intimate. Enjoying their lunch together, they relaxed for a few moments. Then they began to discuss their morning's work. Chrissie reached under the table and put her hand on Janny's knee. Janny shuddered slightly as the tingle from her touch worked its way up her body, making the heat from the day even hotter. Beads of sweat were appearing on her forehead. She dabbed at the sweat with a tissue before it started to roll down her face.

'Oh by the way, what's with the hussy pussy? Is that a new term of endearment for me, my dear darling sleazy slut?'

'If the cap fits, anyway, why are you squirming in your seat love?' Chrissie taunted her.

'You bloody well know why, there is a time and a place you know.'

'Hmmm, I like the way you squirm in your seat it's very sexy.' Chrissie said as she slid her hand further up her knee.

'Pity, I can't reach any further, so that, I'm afraid, is as good as it gets for now.'

'Phew, I can't wait for later, you're such a tease Chrissie.'

'I aim to please.'

The two women finished their lunch, gazing across the table at each other with love and respect in their eyes. Both were anticipating the sex that they would enjoy later that evening.

Janny kissed Chrissie on the cheek as they went their separate ways returning to work for the rest of the day.

*

Mary disembarked from the bus; the terminus in the bus depot was signed as Drayfield. Not too far away from Lockington, it was about four miles. It was far enough to keep her off the police radar, at least for the moment. The voices had been right again.

The heat from the day was still very strong, the sky was clear and the sun was beating down. Mary quickly made her way into the shade, this hot weather didn't suit her much, and her hot flushes always got worse in the heat. She set off towards the local village pub, she was taking a chance but she wanted a meal, and a nice cool refreshing glass of lager would go down well. The voices had told her this would be fine.

In the small darkly lit pub, Mary picked a cosy corner to eat her meal; she had ordered a beef sandwich with homemade chips and a side salad. She thoroughly enjoyed the meal; along with the pint of lager she drank to wash it down. Her stomach was full and she was tired now.

Mary set off again keeping to the back streets and heading towards some privately owned land. She would need to find somewhere sheltered to sleep tonight.

After what seemed to her like a long walk, she finally found a derelict building, it stood back from the main road. It looked disused and run down, but it would at least provide some shelter for her if the weather turned nasty. It would also provide somewhere safe to sleep at night away from any prying eyes. The voices agreed this was a good place to haul up.

Mary entered the building via a battered side door; it was very dark in contrast to the bright sunshine outside. She was temporarily blinded until her eyes gradually adjusted to the dark surroundings. Having spotted a door opposite her entry point she made her way towards it. Through the door there were some concrete steps heading downwards, she descended the steps.

Once downstairs, Mary noticed that the level she was on had lots of small side rooms, one of which had an old hospital bed in it. It would be ideal for her to sleep here. It would have been much better though if it had not resembled the acute psychiatric ward she had just escaped from. At least there was no sadistic medical staff here that wanted to subdue her and keep her from her voices.

The voices told Mary that she would be safe here, they wouldn't lie to her, and they made her feel safe. She looked around to see if there were any sheets for the bed. All she had found so far was an old pair of curtains, they would have to do. If it stayed as warm as this she wouldn't need covers anyway. She shook the curtains to remove any excess dust, and coughed as a cloud of dust filled the air. There was a waterproof mattress on the bed; she placed one of the curtains over it.

'I'll live here for a while, this is free lodgings and shelter for me, and I'm going to make it like a home. It will take a bit of cleaning to make it liveable but this is now all mine.' Mary said aloud to her voices.

The voices listened to her and agreed, she would be safe here, and it was her new home.

Mary wandered up and down the corridor that she had now claimed as her own. She looked around to see if she could find something to clean up her new accommodation. Across from her room was a small utility closet with a sink that actually worked, luckily the water hadn't been cut off. Inside she discovered a few remnants of cleaning fluids and other cleaning aids that had been left there.

She found just across the corridor, a toilet that had a working flush. She had also discovered a bathtub this was pure luxury for her.

'It's just like a hotel, it only needs a bit of a clean-up, this is fantastic.' Mary was very pleased with her new abode.

The voices agreed.

Armed with her cleaning gear, Mary set about cleaning her room. She was humming a song as she cleaned. The voices joined in with the chorus.

4

Janny sat upright in bed, which had disturbed Chrissie who had been in a deep sleep.

'What the fuck?' Chrissie said as she was abruptly brought out of her sleep.

'Sorry.' Janny said as she realized what had happened.

'I didn't mean to wake you up. I've had one of my special dreams and I feel that it's very important that I follow up on it. I saw a male patient on an operating table, he was so frightened and I saw everything that was happening.'

'Go back to bloody sleep and tell me about it in the morning.' Chrissie said as she pulled the sheet up over her head.

Janny settled herself back down in the bed and mumbled apologies as she tried to go back to sleep. The dream had stayed with her for quite some time before sleep finally took over.

The next morning Janny was snoring loudly as Chrissie got out of bed.

'She's becoming a bloody pain.' Chrissie thought.

'She's having those stupid dreams and waking up to remember them. I'll have to have words with her when she gets up.'

Chrissie made some coffee then went for a shower. The morning was quite dull but it was already very warm. The sun was trying to burn off the initial mist of the breaking dawn. A red glow was peering through the clouds; the sun was waiting in the wings. It was preparing to make an appearance, once the mist and clouds had broken. It was going to be very hot.

Janny stirred as the smell of the coffee filtered its way from the kitchen, the aroma invaded her nasal passages. She was tempted out of her sleep as the coffee became so inviting. Once awake, she instantly remembered the dream, it had seemed so real to her last night. It was as real as the reality in the here and now. Very strange.

Sitting at the table together the two women ate their breakfast and drank the coffee. It was a Saturday morning and both women were off work today. It was a luxury they both enjoyed, whenever it happened to fall that way.

'I saw a man in my dream' Janny told her.

'I hope that doesn't mean you're going straight.' Chrissie said sarcastically.

'Of course not silly, I mean I saw a man in one of those special dreams that I've been experiencing. The ones that seem so real and lifelike.'

'Dr Stowers, I think you are suffering from, a Post - shit happens, intensive stress, thingy me bob, do dah what's it, syndrome.'

'You're making that up as you go along'

'Well I'm not a bloody doctor, just a basic, every day, run of the mill DCI, what the hell do I know.'

'You're a very good DCI Chrissie, the best there is in my opinion.'

'Thank you darling.'

They finished breakfast and tidied up.

It had been decided last night that a trip to Doncaster would be nice. It would do them both good to have a change of scenery and it would give them the chance to relax together. They set off in Janny's ford focus to visit the Yorkshire Wild Life Park in Doncaster. They had both thought it would be a nice place to visit on their day off.

'I love the meerkats, they're so funny, and they always remind me of the TV advert' Chrissie said excitedly. 'Let's go and see if the big cats are out.'

They walked leisurely along the path following the signs towards the big cats. It was lovely to see them; they were lucky enough to catch them out and about in the open. It was a warm morning, not too hot so it was the ideal time to see the animals. They were prone to hide away out of the sun if it got too hot.

They saw so many lovely animals as they followed the different signs leading them to various species of wild animals that were all happily living in the wild life park.

'Oh look Janny, a polar bear; they haven't been here very long. Oh look, there's another one diving for fish. Quick, take a photo, have you got your phone handy?'

Janny took out her iPhone and quickly took a photo before the polar bear dived back down into the water. She checked the photo before saving it to her photo stream album; it had captured the moment perfectly.

'Got it Chrissie, its perfect. I'll upload it to Facebook later.'

Janny stood beside Chrissie and took a selfie of them both. She would upload that to Facebook too. Chrissie wasn't too keen on her still being on Facebook, because that's how she had put herself in danger during the last case. Although, she had to accept that as long as Janny didn't do the same stupid things, like meddling and getting the killer to target her, it should be fine. This was the way of the world now. Everyone was on some social media site or other. Janny had both Twitter and Facebook. She was also on Linked In, Instagram and a few other sites. Chrissie wasn't as bothered, she thought it was a time wasting pastime. Having said that, she had to admit it was useful at times.

They stopped for a coffee, resting their legs and feet, admiring the view for a while. It was nice to just relax for a few hours, to get away from the stress of their high profile positions at work.

'Let's go and check out the giraffe's. I absolutely love giraffe's.' Chrissie said as she started to follow the sign that led them towards the giraffe enclosure.

'I'll take some more pictures when we get there.' Janny told her.

The two women were engrossed in the antics of the various animals. They had been acting like a couple of excited school kids. It was a lovely break for them both. They were relaxed, as they appreciated the lovely sunshine. Especially in such lovely surroundings. It was a shame they couldn't stay for longer.

Today had been a good day.

They called in at a Morrison's supermarket on the way home and bought some food and wine. They stocked up on essentials, fresh produce and other items. They had enough to last them at least a week. After loading the car up with the shopping and filling the car with petrol they returned home. Chrissie and Janny went their separate ways to sort out their own houses.

'I'll meet you back at mine in a couple of hours.' Janny said as she dropped Chrissie off outside her house.

*

Alan Denning had been out with some friends. He wasn't totally drunk but he was quite merry. He had downed a fair few lagers and at least a couple of vodka shots. Yes, it had been a good night. He wasn't working or attending med school in the morning, which was just as well. He didn't think he would have been up to studying or working following the night out. Alan didn't indulge too often because he wanted to keep up with his studies. So it was a rare treat to go out with friends from time to time.

After saying goodbye to his friends, he headed towards his digs. He lived in shared student accommodation in Sheffield's City Centre. He was feeling a little tipsy but he managed to walk without falling over and more or less in a straight line. That was promising he thought. As he approached his student digs, someone in a car pulled up just in front of him. He didn't take much notice of it but noticed that the passenger got out. The driver left the engine running. Alan didn't notice the passenger approach. The next thing he was aware of was a sharp prick in his neck. He began to feel groggy; it wasn't long before Alan Denning passed out.

'Oh my God, it must have been a very heavy night.' Alan thought.

He was beginning to regain consciousness, not knowing where he was or how he came to be there. Slowly his memory returned. He gradually remembered leaving the pub. Then he remembered the car and the sharp prick in his neck.   Inside, Alan was starting to panic, something wasn't right. He became aware of a bright light overhead; it was shining down on him, blinding his vision, and stinging his eyes.

'My God, what's happening, who are you? Why have you brought me here? What the hell is going on? Please let me go, I don't know who you are, I haven't done anything to you. Please let me goooooo.' Alan pleaded to the surgeon.

'Don't you worry, you are in safe hands.' The surgeon told him as an assistant began to administer the anaesthetic.

'What the hell has happened? Oh no, please help me, pleaseeee helppppp meeeeeee…..'

Alan Denning closed his eyes and everything went dark.

The make shift operating theatre came to life with all the machines humming and the clatter of surgical tools. The surgeon began the operation. With the help of the small theatre team, the heart transplant was underway.

5

Saturday evening

Mary had been shopping and had brought back a few provisions to get her through the next few days. She was quite contented living there in the old disused hospital. She had brought with her a small radio with some batteries; she inserted the batteries and that now provided her with entertainment and the news. Life was much better here than it was in that God forsaken hospital. The voices agreed with her.

She settled on the bed and listened to the radio, discussing the various news reports with her voices. She took out a packet of crisps and a can of coke. That was her evening sorted.

'Ah, this is the life.' Mary thought.

Mary lit up a cigarette and relaxed as she blew out the smoke. Flicking the excess ash into her make shift ashtray, she talked to the voices and they talked back.

*

DS Mike Hartley was sitting across from his girlfriend DS Sharon Trivett; she had recently been promoted to Detective sergeant. The two had paired up during the 'Stamp Master' case and had been together ever since.

'This meal is absolutely lovely Mike, we must come here again sometime' Sharon told him.

'Yes, it's very nice; it's a lovely way to celebrate my birthday, even better with you here. I couldn't have imagined twelve months ago that my next birthday would be spent in a lovely restaurant with a lovely lady sitting across from me. What more could a man ask for?'

'Well I could think of something that might just finish the night off wonderfully.' Sharon told him smiling broadly with a glint in her eye.

Mike was thirty-four today, he still looked handsome with his designer stubble, and his dark hair. He was slightly overweight but looked good. He looked across at Sharon; she looked gorgeous with her slim figure. Sharon was younger than Mike; she was twenty-six years old and had short dark hair. They had hit it off straight away; the chemistry between them had been there right from the onset of their relationship.

Mike squirmed in his seat as he knocked back the last of the wine in his glass, finishing it in one gulp. They took a taxi back to Mike's place; they started stripping their clothes off as soon as they walked through the door. They stumbled towards the bedroom both sexually aroused to a wine filled frenzy. Banging into things along the way and dropping items of clothing in their wake.

Sharon grabbed hold of his erect penis and guided it inside her. She gasped as he thrust it deeper and harder.

'Happy birthday Mike' Sharon whispered into his ear as he had entered her.

Sharon braced herself for the final thrusts before the orgasm took hold of her. The fire was raging through both their bodies as their orgasms reached their peak. The waves overtook them to a point of no return; they were lost in ecstasy as they had been on numerous occasions since they had first met. The couple finally melted into a fitful and deep sleep as the heat inside them slowly faded.

*

Janny yawned as they sat in her living room sipping on the wine they had opened a few hours ago. They had enjoyed the day out together and now it was their chill out time.

'I'll make breakfast in the morning, omelettes', toast and hot coffee.' Chrissie said.

'That sounds fine to me.' Janny replied as she moved closer to Chrissie.

Chrissie moaned as Janny slid her hand up to that magical place, where everything that was ever important in their lives happened.

Janny parted Chrissies legs and pulled down her

panties.

'Now who's a hussy pussy? Eh? Why aren't you answering me? Eh? Does this feel good girl? Well does it?' Janny teased as she went down on her.

'Oh Yes, Oh Yes, Oh Fuck!!!'

As the sex went on, the orgasms flowed; this is what had kept the couple's relationship alive. This was the reason they were still as close now, as they were on the day they had first met all those years ago.

'I love you darling.' Janny told her as she closed her sleepy eyes.

'I love you too.'

They slept soundly together that night and Janny didn't have any of her special dreams.

Sunday Morning

The smell of eggs and coffee reached Janny's nostrils at around 7am Sunday morning. Chrissie was attempting to make ham and mushroom omelettes for breakfast. She was having some problems. The omelette was going disastrously wrong. It wasn't setting right and the more she stirred it to try and set it the more it scrambled.

Janny walked into the kitchen.

'What's that?' She asked.

'It's supposed to be an omelette, but I'm afraid it's gone a bit wrong.' Chrissie told her.

'Hmmmm.'

'I think I'll have to call it something else now' Chrissie said as she stirred it some more. She added a bit of grated cheese to the concoction.

'It looks like something I would retrieve from the stomach of a post-mortem examination.' Janny said.

'Sod off Janny; I think I'll add this to my cookbook when I decide to create one. I'll call it a scramblette. This could catch on.' Chrissie said with a smile.

'It's an abomination Chrissie, if I was you I'd feed it to the dog.'

'We haven't got a dog.' Chrissie replied.

'They've got one next door, but if you fed it to the dog and it had problems afterwards we could get sued, so I wouldn't bother. I would just put it straight into the bin.'

'Janny, there is nothing in my scramblette to hurt us, so just get it eaten.'

They ate the scramblette and toast and washed it down with the hot coffee. It didn't taste bad; it just looked a bit iffy. The two women sat eating and watching the TV news in the kitchen, there was nothing much to report at the moment.

'What are we going to do today then?' Chrissie asked Janny as she tidied the pots away.

'I don't know, maybe we could go to Meadowhall and check out the perfume shop. I wouldn't mind getting some more Chanel Co.Co. I know it's expensive but I love it. I'd also like to have a nice meal upstairs, it would make up for the scramblette abomination.' Janny said as she turned off the TV.

The two women set off to the Meadowhall shopping Centre. They called in for a coffee in Costa's before starting their shopping spree. Janny bought her perfume and they had a lovely meal upstairs. They were just about to venture into the Mark's and Spencer's food hall when Chrissie's mobile rang.

*

The old hospital was very eerie, it was dark and it seemed as though it had many ghosts from the past all living within these walls. Every corridor gave out its own version of what it once had been. It appears to echo what must have at one time been a hive of activity. Eerie vibes seemed to be emitted from the past decades, which had no doubt housed many medical emergencies. The sounds were almost audible, the visions were almost visible.

Following the transplant, which didn't go entirely to plan. The surgeon was gearing up for a sexual encounter with the nurse. She was very sexy. The nurse was frightened, as she had been on the other previous occasions when the surgeon had visited her. She knew that the surgeon was sadistic and wouldn't hold back on any sexual deviancy that was required to fulfil the ultimate climax. The surgeon was going to get some pleasure from the nurse now. It was one of the perks of being in charge. The nurse wouldn't object, she couldn't.

'This was going to be fun.' The surgeon thought.

The surgeon strolled towards the young nurse's room. There was no fear of the woman identifying who was behind the gown and mask.

'I am in control.' The surgeon said softly, hardly audible.

*

Mary was in her elements, she was listening to the radio and her voices were in discussion with themselves. It was like being at a dinner party. She was very happy; this was much better than being on the ward with all those mentally ill patients. She shouldn't have been there at all. It had all been a big mistake, she was saner than most of the staff there. She felt a bit peckish so she opened up a bag of crisps, mmmm, nice she thought as she munched on the crisps.

'We will be fine here, this place is my home and of course it's yours too my faithful friends.' Mary told the voices.

The voices agreed with her, they continued with their virtual mad hatter's tea party. The radio reported briefly on an escaped patient from a psychiatric hospital, then went on to report a breaking news report of a body being discovered.

'Oh my.' Mary thought. *'That's awful, who would do something like that to another human being.'*

The voices agreed with her, they reassured her and told her not to worry. Nothing bad would happen to her as long as she listened to what they told her. Mary wasn't afraid because the voices were always right, they had always protected her from anything that could harm her. She trusted them totally with her wellbeing and her life.

This place was a Godsend, it was meant to be, this was her sanctuary and her salvation.

'Hallelujah.' Mary shouted out loud.

'Hallelujah.' The voices shouted back.

*

The surgeon was highly sexually aroused and breathing heavily in anticipation of what was about to occur. Everything was going to work out well. The nurse was cowering on the bed, she knew that in the next few minutes the surgeon would walk into her room and violate her in a way no one should ever have to endure. She could hear the approaching footsteps and her heart was pounding in her chest, she thought it would explode it was that strong. As the surgeon entered the room. The young nurse was cowering in a corner.

'Take off your clothes girl and get on the bed.' The surgeon had ordered, in a quiet voice, nothing much beyond a whisper. It was even more menacing because of the softness in the tone.

The young nurse started to strip as the surgeon watched and breathed deeply as the sexual tension built up. A warm sensation was taking hold.

'I am in control.' The surgeon was happy, things were finally going as planned.

The young nurse tried to hold back the tears of despair, she wished she could go back to the life she had before this nightmare. She knew this wasn't going to happen, she knew that within the next few moments she would have to endure extreme terror, pain and perverse sexual torment.

As the surgeon approached her she could feel the vomit trying to rise into her throat, she fought it back as best she could. She could taste it in her mouth as the bile rose. Her mouth was dry one minute and moist with bile the next. She braced herself as the surgeon thrust deep inside her. The nurse bit into her tongue as the sexual deviation began. She could taste the metallic blood along with the sour bile. What had she ever done to deserve this torment? She couldn't comprehend the reasoning behind the sadistic torture that the surgeon was inflicting on her. No one in their right mind would do this.

No words were spoken during the sex attack, she could feel the thrusting penetration and the groping. The nurse had her eyes shut tight now, she couldn't look at the masked attacker it was the stuff nightmares were made of. The nurse wept as the surgeon left her room. This was getting worse. She wished that could escape and go back to the life she had once had. This was worse than death, at least death was final. This nightmare just kept on returning and occurring over and over again.

*

Mary thought she heard something, but the voices were distracting her so she didn't pay it much attention. This was the life, she was happy in her own contented little world. What more could she want? No more awful hospital ward full of weird patients and staff, she didn't have to take the medication that stopped her from listening to the voices. She didn't have to do anything she didn't want to do. This was where she wanted to be. Crunching on crisps and talking to the voices while listening to the radio was quite entertaining.

'Yes.' She said to the voices. 'This is a good place to be, thank you for bringing me here.'

The voices agreed with her. This is a good place to be.

6

Sunday afternoon

Chrissie had received a phone call on her mobile. It was from the station. Apparently a body had been found.

'I'm sure I had a dream about this murder Chrissie, I could help you find the killer if only you would let me.'

'Whatever, we don't even know if it's a murder yet. So please if you don't mind, just do your bloody job and let me do mine.' Chrissie snapped back at Janny.

Chrissie realised that Janny's special dreams were increasingly irritating her. She was beginning to do her head in.

Even so, Chrissie thought Janny looked very fetching in her summer attire, consisting of a light white top with subtle white patterns flowing through it. It complimented her light brown trouser suit.

'What on earth is wrong with you Chrissie?'

'Nothing.'

'It doesn't sound like it.'

'Forget it Stowers, let's concentrate on the job in hand eh? We both should be above all this shit.'

The afternoon sunshine was beautiful; it was enough to lighten anyone's mood. Chrissie and Janny were not as lifted by it as they should have been though.

The phone call that Chrissie had received earlier in Meadowhall was to inform them that a body had been found. Apparently the body had been discovered in a snow salt container bin.

They had returned home and got ready to go to the location where the body had been discovered. They soon arrived at the scene; they could smell the body long before they saw it. Flies were buzzing around the corpse. It was the body of a young male and it appeared that the man had at some stage recently undergone an operation.

'There are stitches here Chrissie, it looks like this bloke has had recent heart surgery. It's the sort of operation I perform regularly.' Janny told her.

'Remind me never to come to you if I need heart surgery. It looks down right iffy to me.'

'I won't know just what procedure was done until I get the body back.' Janny said.

The two women worked the crime scene together with their teams. The forensic team collected as much information and evidence as possible. They sent all the samples to the lab for testing and for any possible leads to the cause of death.

Janny escorted the body to the morgue; she would be doing a post-mortem and a detailed examination report for Chrissie. The forensic team were still working the crime scene along with the police photographer who was taking pictures of the area. They were checking out and recording anything that may be useful for when a suspected killer was found. Also, it would provide sometimes-crucial evidence if a case was taken to court. The teams all worked together doing the jobs that they were highly trained to do

The heat from the afternoon sun had made the smell from the body even worse. Even when the body had been removed, the smell still remained, festering in the heat.

No more nice relaxing Sunday leisure time now, this was a suspicious death and a possible murder case; it took priority over everything else. This was probably going to be a taxing enquiry, one in which both Chrissie and Janny could do without. They were resigned to the fact that this was their vocation; this was what they had both signed up for when they had chosen their career paths. Well someone had to do it. The adrenalin was beginning to kick in.

*

Mary woke up early on Sunday morning; she had a wash and changed her clothes. She washed her dirty clothes in the sink and draped them over a bed frame. She used this as a makeshift clothes-drying rack. Then she ate a few biscuits for breakfast. She lit up a cigarette and blew the smoke out in a long stream. Flicking her ash into an old rusty kidney dish, this was her makeshift ashtray.

'I must get some more cigarettes; I don't want to run out of them. I would totally lose it if I did.' She thought.

She'd tried those new-fangled electronic cigarettes. She didn't like them at all. Too much faffing around with them and they didn't have the same satisfying effect that a real cigarette has. Even though it is supposed to be much safer to use e-cigs than real ciggies, she'd decided to stick to her trusty cancer sticks. They had a much more satisfying and calming effect on her, and she needed to be calm right now. She had noticed her smoker's cough was quite bad in the mornings though.

'Well if it gets any worse I'll have to reconsider using the e-cigs but for now I'll stick to the real things.' She thought.

Mary took another drag of her cigarette, the smoke caught in her throat causing her to cough. It hurt her throat. She was fine after the first few puffs. It cleared her tubes out. She flicked the ash into the kidney dish.

Mary drank some water from the tap in the sink. The voices had told her the water was safe to drink and of course they were always right.

'I must go and buy myself a mug.' She told the voices. The voices agreed.

Following her evening last night, listening to her

radio and conversing with her voices she was quite contented and happy. This was the best she had felt for a long time. The years she had spent in and out of the psychiatric hospital wards had been horrendous. She didn't intend to ever return there, the voices had told her she would be safe as long as she listened to their warnings and advice. Mary had no reason to disbelieve them. She was warm and dry, she had food, and water and most importantly, she had a roof over her head.

Mary went out to buy a few more provisions; taking extra care not to draw any attention to herself. The voices had told her not to use shops too close to where she was squatting. They had warned her not to stay in a shop too long. So she went into the shop and bought her provisions, then got out as quickly as possible with a minimum of fuss.

'Ah, this is the life, it's better than I could ever have imagined.' Mary told the voices.

The voices agreed with her.

Mary Smithe smiled; she hadn't smiled like this in such a long time. The voices told her it was ok to smile. She switched on her little battery operated portable radio, some easy listening music came out of the very small and tinny speaker. But to Mary this was the height of technology; she thanked the listening voices for helping her. The voices were smiling too.

'I'm going to have so much fun here with you guys.'

The voices agreed.

Mary reached into her makeshift food cupboard; she took out a bar of chocolate and began to indulge in one of life's more comforting pleasures.

7

Sunday evening

The two women were watching the TV. After a few awkward moments, Chrissie channelled her energy into popping the cork on a bottle of wine. That seemed to do the trick; both women were snuggling up together on the couch beginning to feel amorous again.

Chrissie slipped her hand into the opening of Janny's dressing gown. The night was still relatively young and their passion was still very high, despite the conflicting emotions running through them.

Tomorrow was going to be the beginning of a murder enquiry. Chrissie's line of enquiry would all depend on the findings Janny found following the post-mortem.

Chrissie didn't envy Janny's job, it was something that would certainly turn her stomach over. Janny was used to it she had performed so many of them. It wouldn't be too long before they discovered what had caused the death of the young man.

'Tomorrow I'll be making an early start on the post-mortem.' Janny said as she pulled up her panties.

'Oh you are such a romantic darling.' Chrissie replied.

'We really could have done without having to solve another mystery death so soon after the Stamp Master case.' Janny told her.

'The fact is Janny, we have our jobs to do and the nature of the work we do is usually very taxing. If we didn't want to do it we wouldn't be in the line of work we are in would we? So let's not worry too much about what could be and concentrate on the here and now.'

Chrissie sighed as she picked up her glass and downed the rest of its contents. She picked up the wine bottle and refilled both their glasses as she turned up the volume on the TV. The late evening news was reporting on a local woman who had gone missing from an acute psychiatric ward. She hadn't been found yet and was considered to be dangerous. The newsreader told the public that if they came across the woman, they should report it to the police and in no way should they try to confront her.

'Why haven't we found this woman who has escaped from the hospital? Good grief, if I can't even apprehend a missing person! What chance do I have with anyone else?'

'Chrissie, after what we've been through, it's a wonder we're still capable of doing our jobs at all. You are a brilliant detective and I am a very good surgeon, and forensic medical examiner, we excel at what we do. We will come through this no matter what happens; you know that deep down inside. It's what we do; it's what we have specialised in. Nothing and no one can change that, we are both strong willed women, we will not fall or fail in doing what comes natural to us. We are the best and we shouldn't think anything less of ourselves. Never forget that!'

'You're right of course, but I don't feel the same as I did before. It is probably all in my mind but that doesn't change how I feel.'

'You'll be fine Chrissie; it's what you do. You are like me in that respect. We live for our jobs, our work controls our lives. We are both professional people who have channelled our lives to serve, heal and protect anyone who is in need of our help. We'll get through whatever life throws at us.'

'Hmm, it's time to go to bed now darling let's get some beauty sleep eh.' Chrissie said as she led the way.'

8

Monday morning

The day started quite mildly at first. Chrissie was up first and Janny followed shortly afterwards.

'I'm going in soon, I really want to make an early start on the post-mortem as soon as possible.'

'Yes, it's going to be a long day. We'd better get a move on.'

Following a quick breakfast, the two women set off to work. Janny had the post-mortem examination to perform. Chrissie had an incident board to set up in the major incident room.

It was nice and warm outside but not too hot, the sun hadn't broken through the clouds yet. It was a very pleasant time of the day. People were setting out and going to their various locations. Some were making their way to work; others were out enjoying the comfortable warmth before the sun made it uncomfortably unpleasant. It was going to be another hot and humid day according to the weather forecast.

*

Mike nudged Sharon as he got out of bed.

'What time is it?' Sharon slurred as she blinked away the sleep.

'It's time to get up and get ready for work.' Mike told her as he reached over and kissed her.

'Last night was amazing darling, I love you so much Mike.'

'I love you too babe, come on and get up now detective sergeant Trivett, we've both got jobs to go to my dear.'

'Spoil sport, can't you squeeze a quickie in.'

'Hmm, you temptress let me be, before I get to the point of no return.'

Mike was aware of his extreme happiness. This was all down to his relationship with Sharon. He had all but given up on trying to find a worthy partner. He was hurt and insecure following the collapse of his marriage. He was not interested in a long-term relationship. That was of course until Sharon had come along and completely stole his heart away. He was very glad that fate had intervened and put some meaning and pleasure back into his life. He was a little afraid that the bubble might burst, but for now he was revelling in the wondrous feelings he was now experiencing.

Mike reached the point of no return and gave in to Sharon's seduction.

'Is this squeezed in quickly enough for you?'

Mike said as he pushed his hard shaft inside Sharon, pumping away quickly to reach a climax.

'Ok, whiz kid, how's about giving me a workout too?'

He managed to slow down and they soon settled into a satisfying rhythm that suited them both. They climaxed with the rising hot throbbing sensations that completely engulfed them. It took them both to the place of extreme ecstasy that always accompanied an orgasm.

They both enjoyed and relished the moment. It was a wonderful start to the day before the harsh reality of work set in.

*

It was a typical Monday morning, most people hated going into work following the weekend. Those Monday morning blues had always created a bit of a downer for most people. For Chrissie and Janny it was a way of life, they had built their relationship around their work. The couple had been through so much together and although they don't share a home together, they shared a bed together almost every night. Their independence was never compromised, so it suited them both.

Following breakfast, the two women went about their work business. Setting off to two different locations.

Janny set off to the morgue; she was going to be busy doing a post-mortem. Chrissie made her way to the Police Headquarters to set up an incident room for the imminent inquiry.

'Can you get me Cheryl Teal on the phone please Sally?' Chrissie asked her bubbly secretary.

Sally, DCI Chrissie Charles's secretary was her biggest support in the unit. Chrissie knew that she could totally rely on her. She brought a lively freshness into the sometimes-depressing areas of the police station.

'I'm on it.' Sally told her.

Chrissie asked Mike to look into the missing person cases again. There was probably something they had missed somewhere along the line. She was especially concerned about Mary Smithe the escaped schizophrenic patient. She should have turned up by now. She was more than likely hiding out somewhere. This was one of the things she would like to talk to Cheryl about.

Although the adrenalin was beginning to kick in now, Chrissie couldn't help feeling apprehensive. This would be her first murder investigation since the horrific Stamp master case. A shudder rippled through her body, as if someone had just walked over her grave. She hoped that it wouldn't be a reality.

The phone on Chrissie' desk rang.

'I've got Cheryl on the line, putting her through.' Sally told her.

*

Janny was performing a post-mortem on the young man they had found in the salt bin. She did the usual full body checks before preparing to remove the internal organs.

After cutting the Y incision into the body, the first thing she noticed when she opened him up made her gasp. She took a deep breath as she realised what she was looking at.

'Oh my God.' She uttered as she breathed out. 'Chrissie is going to have kittens when I tell her.'

This wasn't going to be a straightforward case. But was there ever such a thing as a straightforward case?

Janny continued with the post-mortem examination, making sure she checked the body thoroughly, it was very important not to miss anything. It could make all the difference between finding a killer or not.

Janny carefully inspected the victim's body for wounds of any kind. During the inspection she noticed a small puncture wound in the man's neck. That could have possibly been caused by a hypodermic needle. She took photographs of all the various body parts and the fact there was an absence of a heart. So the operation he had undergone was not heart surgery as such but a complete removal of the heart. So weird. She also documented the possible needle mark in his neck. After documenting all her findings she began to write the post-mortem report.

'This is going to be very complicated, got to stay focused girl and check everything.' Janny thought to herself.

Samples taken from the site had been transported to the toxicology lab for testing. The detective work had now begun.

Janny dreaded telling Chrissie about her findings. She would have to break the news to her gently because Chrissie had really changed since the stamp master case. In fact, if the truth be known, they had both changed, but neither of them for the better. PTSD (Post Traumatic Stress Disorder) had taken its toll on them both. They could have done without this challenging case so relatively soon afterwards.

Janny was getting one of her stress related headaches. She could feel the pressure building up inside her head.

'Well, that's a good start to a Monday morning, I wonder how it will progress from here?' Janny thought.

She knew that she had to let Chrissie know as soon as possible, the pain in her head increased as she thought about it. She wasn't looking forward to breaking the news to her. Janny decided she would need to take some painkillers for her headache before it got any worse.

Janny was experiencing a fight or flight feeling brought on by her anxiety. Knowing full well that if she were given the choice she would fly away without hesitation. It wasn't an option, so she fought against all her negative thoughts. After popping some pills for her headache, Janny reached for her phone. She could feel her hands tremble as she called Chrissie.

Chrissie looked at the caller ID on her mobile. It was Janny.

'Hi Janny, how's the post-mortem examination coming along?'

Janny took in a deep breath.

'You are not going to believe what I've discovered Chrissie. The post-mortem uncovered that our victim had no heart.'

'What do you mean no heart, that is impossible isn't it?'

'I mean the victim's heart has been surgically removed from his body. He was dead before he was dumped where we found him.'

'Bloody hell Janny ……'

'I know Chrissie, I was dreading telling you but you need to know that this murder investigation, is a very weird one. I'm sorry, it's the last thing we need right now.'

'Hey it's not your fault, but who in their right mind would want to remove a man's heart with a precise surgical procedure and then dump his body?'

'At the moment I haven't got a clue, but I'm going to send you a full report of my findings. I'm staying here for a while to recheck the body, just in case I missed something important. I'll meet up with you later and we can go through the details.'

'Ok, keep me posted Janny.' Chrissie sighed as she finished the call.

'Oh no not again, I haven't got over the stamp master murders yet. I can sense that this is going to be another horrendous and challenging case.' Chrissie thought.

9

Monday morning

Chrissie briefed her team and put procedures into action. The white board would once again be the centrepiece in the major incident room. A feeling of Déjà vu and nausea came over her.

The feeling of dread ran through her body causing her to shake, the tremors in her hands were making her even more nervous. She fought hard to control the shakes and tried to regain her composure. She knew that she was going to need her wits about her if she had any hope of finding the killer.

'Right Chrissie, come on, get a bloody grip. You can handle this.' She thought to herself. *'You have to handle this. You have no choice, you are the bloody DCI for God's sake.*

Sally Williams walked into the meeting room where Chrissie and Cheryl Teal the Criminal Psychologist were seated. She had a tray with hot coffee and a plate of assorted biscuits. Sally placed the tray between them and left quietly.

Chrissie looked up at her secretary as she entered.

'Thank you Sally, much appreciated.'

Cheryl thanked her too.

'Thank you for coming to see me at such short notice Cheryl, I'd like you to help me build a profile for this killer. It's a particularly gruesome murder as you can see from the pictures. The post-mortem revealed a shocking revelation when Janny discovered that the victim was minus his heart. Apparently he had undergone a recent heart operation, had his heart removed, then he was stitched up.'

'Oh my God, how awful.' Cheryl Teal said as she toyed with a loose strand of hair that had escaped its tie back.

Cheryl is the criminal psychologist for the unit, a highly qualified member of the police team. At thirty-four years old, she has a slim figure and long black hair. She profiled suspects and also provided some insight into the personality of any potential suspects. She would often compare the killer traits with her previous cases. This gave her a general idea of what type of killer had murdered any victims that were found.

Cheryl had a sip of her coffee and took a bite out of a custard cream biscuit while she continued to gather her thoughts.

'I'm going to need a bit more time to make a detailed report. But it goes without saying really that the person who removed the heart must have had some sort of medical knowledge. It could be either a working medic or a surgeon, or it could be someone who is pissed off at having been struck off. Or it could possibly be a trainee in the later stages of their training. As far as the profile is concerned, I would suggest that this person has an agenda of some sort. Something has motivated the killer to perform such an intricate operation. Enough for the killer to go to the lengths of removing the victim's heart. It could be that this person is disappointed with the health service or something could have happened to someone close. I'm sorry it's so vague but there's not much to go on yet.'

Cheryl reached for another biscuit, finished the biscuit and continued.

'There is also a possibility that more than one person may be involved in the killing. The person performing the operation would in all probability have had some sort of assistance during the procedure.'

Chrissie asked Cheryl her opinion about the escaped psychiatric patient. Cheryl promised to write up a full report on Mary Smithe as soon as possible along with a preliminary profile on the heartless killer.

Chrissie went back into the incident room following her meeting with Cheryl. She contacted DI James Barrow and DS Mike Harding along with newly promoted DS Sharon Trivett. They were all out gathering information. There was nothing new to report from them.

DCI Chrissie Charles had recently recruited a new member of staff on her team. Constable Amy Campbell who had been appointed to replace DS

Trivett. PC Campbell had appeared to be enthusiastic, smart and level headed so far. Chrissie had introduced her to the rest of the team on her arrival.

Before PC Campbell started work, Chrissie had started a personal staff file on her as she did with all her staff. It was always handy to have details of her staff. Phone contacts, addresses etc. were always useful to have at hand. The main personnel files were stored and filed in the human resources department.

The phone rang in the incident room, Chrissie picked it up.

'I've got the Commissioner on the line for you.' Sally told her.

'Ok, put him through Sally.'

'Hello David, what can I do for you?'

'What's all this about a murder eh? What have you got for me? I'll need all the details as and when they come in. You understand that don't you? I'll have to give a press release as soon as possible but I'll stall with the details until we have something concrete to report. I can be doing without this, especially following the last major murder incident we had. I know I can count on you to keep me in the loop but be very careful what you say to the press.'

'Everything we have on the case so far is in the report I faxed to you earlier. There hasn't been any more developments as yet. If I get anything more I'll fax it straight through to you. As far as the press is concerned it goes without saying, I'll certainly keep it as low profile as I can until we know more.'

Police Commissioner David Maroni was panicking already, he wasn't ready for this case anymore than Chrissie or Janny was. There was a killer out there and no one would rest now until that killer was found.

'Shit, I can do without him on my back again. It's been quiet and even boring over the last few months. Now it's all happening again. I hope I can cope with it. I know I will, but it's not like it was before. The bloody stamp master has a lot to answer for. Now, get a grip and do your job.' Chrissie told herself.

She picked up the phone and got hold of DS Mike Hartley.

'Mike can you check missing persons for me please? You'll need to check out anyone who has been reported missing over the last few months or so. I have a hunch that there may be a few on that missing person list who could be connected to our enquiries. I need information, and anything else that might be relevant to this case.'

'Will do ma'am, I'll let you know when I've done the checks and I'll get the details back to you as soon as I have them.'

'Thanks Mike, let me know when you've got a list of the missing persons, then we can try to trace any relevant ones.'

There was one missing person that they would need to know the whereabouts of as soon as possible, and that was Mary Smithe. She was at the top of the list so far.

Mike got back to Chrissie to inform her that the body they had found had been identified.

'The victim was Alan Denning a nineteen year old med student, he was reported missing by his roommates when he failed to return from a night out. I'll get the details to you a.s.a.p.'

'Thanks Mike, great work.' Chrissie told him.

She knew this was going to be a busy and stressful day, but at least she wouldn't get bored

10

Monday afternoon

Janny had finally completed her post-mortem examination on Alan Denning. Her newly recruited forensic scientist had helped her.

The new man, David Harris; had a long string of very good qualifications. He was already proving himself to be a promising member of the forensic team. David was finalising the report Janny had asked him to prepare for her. It would soon be ready to give to Chrissie.

David was happy to be working alongside Dr Janny Stowers; she lived up to the reputation she had earned. The twenty five year old, blond hared, blue-eyed scientist had a bit of crush on Janny, but he knew she was gay and that her partner was DCI Chrissie Charles. That was definitely a no go area. He also knew about the stamp master case. When he was taken on, David had looked on the Internet for any information about his new boss. It was very interesting to say the least.

David had been a newly graduated surgeon, when he had decided to specialise in the field of forensic science. He had acquired on hands experience in many different areas of performing surgical operations. He had spent the last four years of his medical training qualifying for the many specialised areas of his career. This was just one of them.

He was certainly dedicated to his vocation, that's what Janny had liked about him when they had interviewed him for the post. It was becoming a rare commodity these days. Janny had gone out of her way to ensure that he would be trained to the highest standards. David Harris deserved it; he had obviously worked very hard to get to this stage in his very promising career. Janny was pleased with her choice when she'd set him on. So far he had proved to be a great assist to the team.

Janny was beginning to get hunger pangs, she decided to visit Chrissie at the police headquarters and suggest that they go to get some lunch. Knowing Chrissie, she would have forgotten to eat.

On her arrival, Janny went straight to Chrissie's office. Chrissie was sitting at her desk perusing a report that Cheryl had faxed through. It just reiterated what they had discussed earlier that morning.

'Hey gorgeous, do you fancy going to get a bite to eat, I want to talk to you about the post-mortem results and I'm starving.'

'Oh is it that time already? Doesn't time fly when you're having fun. I've been so absorbed in setting up this enquiry that I haven't given lunch a second thought.'

'Well grab your things; we are both in need of some sustenance to keep our strength up. It will help to keep our minds focused on what we're doing. We're no good to anyone if we can't do our jobs through lack of concentration.'

'Yes you're right, where shall we go? Pub or café?'

*

They had opted for the pub.

Sitting in a recess of the Halfpenny pub, Chrissie and Janny were eating a sandwich and drinking their espresso coffees. The cosy corner was ideal for eating, and for privately reflecting on the case so far.

'Well all I can say is, here we go again.' Chrissie said after Janny had explained in more detail what the post-mortem had revealed.

'I was dreading telling you Chrissie, I knew it would be a shock, it was for me.'

'I've got the incident room and white board set up, I'd like to get this case solved as soon as possible. At least now we know who the victim is which is a good start.'

'Yes, we have a starting point, hopefully it will lead us to the finishing point.' Janny said.

In the bar area sat Ryan Guilder, he had been arrested as a suspect in the stamp master case. The large man had unfortunately fitted the profile of the killer. Ryan had tried to put the whole stressful mess behind him, but he still had bad memories.

Ryan was sitting with his drinking mate Chippy

Miles, they chatted as they drank. Dougie Collins walked into the pub and ordered a beer. He was also one of the group of drinking mates. Dougie, a plumber, usually met them at the pub if he wasn't too far away at lunchtime. Sometimes he would have a quick drink with his mates after finishing work at teatime. Then he would go home to his wife Trisha and their two daughters.

They had all been shocked and affected by the horrific murders. The stamp master had turned out to be one of their former-drinking pals. Jacob Taylor had been one of the lads until he had gotten sick and started killing. That was all in the past now, the pals tried not to dwell on it too much. Easier said than done though.

'Hey, have you lot heard about that body they've found?' Ryan asked his pals.'

'I heard something on the local news, they didn't give much away though.' Chippy replied.

'Well, as far as I know, there was a body found in one of those yellow snow salt bins. Apparently it's suspicious, so that means that it's probably a murder.'

'Oh shit, as though we haven't had our fair share of them in the past.' Chippy told his pals.

The friends discussed the possible murder whilst they continued to devour their food and drinks.

Chrissie and Janny had finished their sandwiches. The meal had been very nice; it filled a hole and would last them now until the evening.

Chrissie's mobile rang as they were leaving the pub. Mike had been checking the missing person files and there were a few on his list that he thought would need further investigation. He passed the information on to Chrissie.

'Thanks Mike, can you follow up on the ones that need our attention. I'll leave that up to you for now. Let me know if you need any back up.'

Chrissie returned to the station, there was a major crime to solve. Her heart felt heavy at the thought of what might lie ahead of them.

Janny went back to the station with her; there were a few things they would need to discuss. It was always better to discuss them face-to-face. As they walked in through the station door a young attractive woman pc was standing just in front of them. Chrissie introduced the young woman.

'Janny this is Amy Campbell, she is Sharon Trivetts' replacement now that Sharon that has been promoted to Detective Sergeant. She's going out in the field today to help DI James Barrow with a few enquiries.'

'Pleased to meet you Amy, I'm Dr Janny Stowers, cardio vascular specialist, consultant and medical examiner. I hope you're settling in ok. They're not a bad lot here, quite a good team.'

'I think I'll be fine thanks. Just getting to know

the ropes at the moment. Lovely to meet you.'

James put his head around the door summoning Amy. Sorry I've got to dash. See you again soon.' Amy said as she made her way towards the door.

'Amy seems nice. I've got a new forensic scientist working for me. David Harris, he's very good. No problems so far. I don't know much about him personally, but his credentials are outstanding. It's always strange for a new member of staff when they are just joining the team.' Janny told Chrissie.

'You just stay away from the new bloke's outstanding credentials girl. Well then, shall we have a look at the white board and see what we've got so far?'

'Better make a start I suppose. I've got the post-mortem report here with me, the main details can go on the board too.' Janny said as she produced the document out of her briefcase.

Janny passed the post-mortem report to Chrissie along with a toxicology report.

The toxicology report had found traces of:

Suxamethonium chloride
Sodium Pentathol

'The Suxamethonium induces muscle relaxation and the Sodium Pentathol is also known as the truth drug. Best known as an intravenous drug for anaesthesia.' Janny explained.

Chrissie thanked her and pinned them on the whiteboard with some graphic pictures and all the other information they had gathered so far. It would gradually fill up during the course of the investigation.

*

Monday afternoon

Mary had just returned from a visit to a supermarket. She had gone to buy some food; she had put on some clean clothes, to make herself look respectable. Mary smiled; she had attempted to make herself look as normal as possible. No way did she want to attract any unwanted attention to herself. She had been very lucky so far, the voices had warned her of any possible pitfalls, so all was good at the moment.

Mary unloaded the carrier bag of provisions, this should be enough to last her a few days. The voices told her to stay here at least for now. Something was bothering her; she thought she'd heard something coming from the floor above her last night. She didn't know what it was, but the voices had told her not to investigate, not yet.

She obeyed the voices without question they always knew best. It was worrying Mary though. Was there someone else squatting here? If so, would it be safe for her to stay here? She would have to be extra careful and stay alert until she found out more. She would also need a weapon in case she had to defend herself. The voices told her not to panic but to stay alert. Mary agreed.

*

Monday afternoon

Amy Campbell was one of the constables working on the case. She was sitting in the incident room along with the other officers in the afternoon briefing.

Janny talked them through the forensic test results that had come through. Chrissie informed the team of their assignments for their shift. There was so much work to do, lots of information to gather, along with many hours of footwork.

Following the briefing, the team set out to their respective locations. Amy walked over to Janny.

'Hello, again.' Amy said to Janny.

'Hiya.' Janny replied.

'How are you settling in?' Ok I hope.'

'I like it here, it's like being part of a big family. And now we have a murder case to solve, it's so exciting.'

Amy told Janny excitedly as she stared into her eyes. Chrissie had noticed the way Amy was staring at Janny and didn't like the way she leered.

'Glad you like it here, but there's plenty of work for you to, do so hadn't you better be getting on with it?' Chrissie told Amy.

'Oh yes, sorry.' Amy said as she made her way

out of the incident room.

'That was a bit harsh, wasn't it Chrissie?'

'Not really, I can't be doing, with any slackers on the team. She needs to start as she means to go on. Give a new recruit an inch and they'll take a yard. I know how to handle them, I've had enough of them in the past.'

'Still, I think you was a little hard on her, she was only saying hello to me.'

'We're working on a murder case, I haven't got the time for all this bullshit.'

Chrissie walked out of the incident room and left Janny standing there in a bewildered state. Janny couldn't understand why Chrissie was suddenly becoming hostile towards her; they had always been so close. This wasn't the way they had been before the trauma of the Stamp Master case. Something had happened and it had changed everything they had once shared together. Janny didn't know what to do about it; she hoped they could sort themselves out. She hoped this new murder enquiry wasn't going to make things worse. Now all she could do was work and hope that things would settle down again at some stage. She just wanted things to get back as near as possible to the way they had been before.

Chrissie felt guilty, she hadn't intended to have a go at Amy. It wasn't like her to be so rude to her staff. She had been watching the way Amy had looked at Janny and for the first time ever in their relationship, Chrissie realised that she had felt the pangs of jealousy.

Something had started to go wrong with their relationship, there were cracks appearing in what was once a strong and solid partnership between them. Chrissie was feeling sad and depressed at the thought of losing Janny. Surely it would never come to that. Not after being together for so long, what they had between them was special, something to hang onto and fight for.

Chrissie was only half listening to the voice of D.I Barrow as he recited what the he knew about the case. She could hear his voice in the background, her own thoughts were running riot, drowning out what James was saying.

'What do you reckon? I've just asked Janny to look into my theory. If we can get an early start on this case, it would give us an advantage. Right now it's the only thing we've got.'

'Er hmm, yes, that's fine James, by all means, follow your line of enquiry. I've got one or two lines of enquiry to follow myself. So let's just leave it there for the time being and see what evolves.'

Chrissie's mind was wandering; she hadn't been taking much notice of what James had said. She was too preoccupied with her thoughts. Mostly about Janny's weird behaviour. Mainly she was worried and disturbed about those strange, so called dreams she was having.

'Any progress with the missing psychiatric patient?' Chrissie asked him.

'We've had a few vague sightings, and one or two phone calls. We're looking into those right now. So far we've got nothing substantial to go on as yet. I'll let you know what transpires. if anything comes from them. Leave it with me.' He told D.C.I. Chrissie Charles as he pulled himself out of the comfortable chair he was sitting in.

'So far, so good.' James thought.

He picked up a copy of the Sun newspaper and let all the active clues run around in his head for a while. It was always manic during a current murder investigation. James was due for a break, so he headed off to the café and ordered a strong coffee to help to keep him awake.

*

The surgeon had acquired most of the equipment from the Internet. It was a good place to find almost everything and anything. Because of the nature of the specialist items the surgeon would need, it was important to have all the equipment in place before beginning. It had taken some time to arrange, but eventually the time had come, the surgeon now had everything.

It might not be ideal, but at least it would suffice. It would have to do; there was no other option. The surgeon smiled, it was going to work, it had to.

11

Two weeks later

David Blackstock was tired, following a very busy day in the classroom. He had been teaching maths to his unwilling and disinterested students. After school he had marked some of the day's classwork before heading off home. He was now living with his parents following his separation from his wife Emma a few months ago.

He set off home; his mind was wandering. David was pre-occupied with the many incidents and problems the day had produced.

He hadn't noticed the black range rover pull up just in front of him. He didn't see the person who got out of the car and walked towards him. It was too late once David had realized what was happening, to stop the drugged hypodermic needle being thrust into his neck. David Blackstock was very groggy as he was pushed into the back of the vehicle.

As David gradually regained consciousness, he vaguely remembered the sharp stabbing pain in his neck before passing out.

'What on earth had happened? What is that bright light? Who is that?' David thought as a sense of dread and panic set in.

He tried frantically to free himself from the table

he discovered he was strapped to. David was about to have some sort of operation. He didn't know why and he didn't know what surgical procedure was about to take place. What he did know was, that he shouldn't be here; whatever was about to take place in this old decrepit operating theatre wasn't legal.

The surgeon was looming over him.

'Please, what's happening? Please tell me what's going on.' David pleaded with the surgeon.

The surgeon didn't reply, but continued to prepare the instruments for the operation, laying them out in neat lines on the trolley.

This isn't right, I've been kidnapped. I was brought here for God only knows what. I have to get out of here. I must get out now before it's too late.' David thought as the anaesthetic began to take him away.

David Blackstock didn't think anymore.

*

Chrissie was still wading her way through all the paperwork that the murder of Alan Denning had produced. The many interview reports and forensic reports were drifting in at a steady rate. Chrissie had updated the incident board each time a new report or point of interest had occurred.

Her stomach had started to rumble making her aware that she was ready for a break. Janny had called her a few minutes ago to suggest they meet up for lunch. That had probably kick started her hunger pangs. Chrissie tidied up her desk before Janny arrived. The two women headed off to Jack's café for a quick bite to eat.

'How's it going Chrissie?' Janny asked.

'Well, I've had better days, I'm just wading my way through all the reports as usual. I'm trying to find a clue or two from what I have received so far. I hope I can find something that will point us in the right direction. Not easy, I've got to keep following up on all the leads. One little piece of evidence might just lead us to the killer. It's knowing which piece of the jigsaw collected from the evidence is the correct one.'

'Well, you've been there before not just the last case but others too. You are a dab hand at this Chrissie, it may take a little while, but you'll get there in the end. I have every faith in you darling.'

'Thanks Janny, I really need some positive vibes at the moment. I've no idea yet who the possible suspects may be. I just hope it will fall into place soon.'

'I'm sure it will Chrissie, try not to get too stressed over it. You need to stay focused and in charge now.'

'What are you saying my sweetness? That I'm not in control? Pick your words carefully my dear. I won't be responsible for my actions if you don't.

What with me not being in control and all that.'

'I didn't mean it like that and you know it. Anyway, what shall we have for lunch I'm starving?'

The two women ate salad sandwiches washed down with latte coffees. They talked about the case for a little while, then they both returned to the police station.

Chrissie returned to her office after they had arranged to meet up after work. They had decided to go for a quick evening meal before returning to Chrissie's house for the night.

Janny went into the toilet while she was still in the police headquarters. She had popped in because she needed a pee before returning to the hospital. She was washing her hands when pc Amy Campbell walked in. For some reason unbeknown to Janny, she was beginning to feel uneasy in Amy's presence. Janny continued to wash her hands, then dried them under the hot air blower. She had grunted a quick hi to Amy as she walked in. Amy stood close to her, too close, she was invading her space. She was aware of her eyes staring at her as she finished drying her hands.

'Hi Janny, I've just been changing an ink jet cartridge on the printer, I've got ink on my hands.' Amy told her.

'Hi Amy, I hope you are settling in ok. I'll see you soon.' Janny told her as she headed out of the door.

She felt relieved when she had left the building. She had no idea why she felt this way. She didn't know why she felt so threatened by the young woman. Was she trying to deliberately intimidate her? Janny was beginning to wonder what her intentions were. She felt that there was definitely a hidden agenda here.

*

Chrissie was sitting at her desk when the news of a second victim was brought to her attention.

'Oh no.' Chrissie thought. 'This is not happening, not again. I was hoping it was just a one off.'

Although deep down, she had been half expecting it, it was still a shock. She contacted her detective team and informed Janny. Janny arranged for her forensic team to attend and collect any evidence. The teams of detectives, photographers and forensic scientists headed to the crime scene.

The body had been discovered by a ward orderly behind some large bins in a waste area at the Lockington Royal Infirmary. Janny was already at the hospital so she didn't have far to go.

Chrissie met up with DS Mike Hartley at the hospital.

'Who discovered the body?' Chrissie asked DS Hartley.

'Bob Dorchester he's a ward orderly, came out to

bring some clinical waste. I've taken his statement.'

'Where's DI Barrow? Why isn't he here?'

'He's on his way ma'am, should be here anytime now.'

'Ok, let's take a look at the body. Have the forensic team and Dr Stowers arrived yet?'

'Yes, they're already collecting and bagging. The hospital waste area is just over there.'

Chrissie followed Mike to the crime scene.

'What can you tell me Janny? Is this the same as the first body?'

'Looks like it, the victim has a similar operation scar. We won't know until I've done the post mortem whether or not he still has a heart.'

'Can't wait, watch this space.' Chrissie said sarcastically.

'I'm sure I saw this man in one of my dreams, if I remember rightly he was on his way home from school when he was kidnaped.' Janny told a cringing Chrissie.

'Oh no not again, you are totally doing my head in with all this shit. Why would this man be coming home from bloody school? He's a bit too old for school I would have thought.'

'I'm sorry if it upsets you, but I really do think I could help you if you would only take me seriously.' Janny told her. 'Well like it or not, I did see this man in one of my dreams. I did see him walking home from school. I think it will be significant in some way once we know who he is. I also saw the operating theatre, which in my view left a lot to be desired. The person, or surgeon performing the operation was dressed in scrubs so I couldn't give you a description. But if anything I dream could be of help, you really should take it seriously. I haven't got a clue as to how this works, all I know is that I can foresee some things. So darling, if I were you I would at least listen to what I have to say. It might even help you.'

'I'd much prefer it if you would stick to your proper job and use scientific evidence to collaborate your views in this investigation. It looks like it's going to be a serial killing spree to me. What I would really like to know is how he died, what the background information is and if he had anything in common with the first victim. If you don't mind, that would be more beneficial to me.' Chrissie told her in an abrupt manner.

'Chrissie, please, at least think about what I've told you. Don't rule it out. Of course I'll do my proper job, as you call it, but if this other way is helpful, don't shrug it off. That's all I ask, keep an open mind.'

'Get a blood grip Janny, I've never known you like this. You actually believe all this shit you're pumping out. I can't believe that you would even consider this garbage, it's so unreal and so far away from how you used to think. All I want from you, is for you to do your job in the normal and proper manner, nothing else if you don't mind.'

'I'm sorry you feel this way, I've done lots of research on NDE's which is Near Death Experiences. I know something has happened to me since mine and I can't explain it, but I know something unusual is happening. It could be extremely useful, especially once I know how to channel it properly. I know some of it has actually happened already. You just won't acknowledge it, I was sceptical like you at first. There comes a point where the facts far outweigh the scepticism. So believe in it or not, something important is being channelled through me. Like I said it could be really useful in helping you to solve this case. Just don't ignore it.'

'Whatever.' Chrissie said as she walked away.

The forensic team were busy collecting information along with the photographic evidence. They were almost ready to move the corpse to the morgue.

Once the body had been moved, Janny had booked in the post-mortem for tomorrow morning. She would have liked to have fitted it in before that, but it wasn't possible. She knew that Chrissie would be eager to get the results.

DCI Chrissie Charles returned to the station, she was in her office when her mobile informed her of an incoming text message.

'Love and Peace my sexy darling.

Let's go to the Ship for our evening meal. We can talk and eat. I'm doing the PM in the morning and I'll let you know all the details as soon as I can.

Luv Jan xxxx.'

Chrissie sent a text back.

'OK see you later darling.
Luv Chris xxxx.'

Chrissie put up some graphic pictures of the latest victim on her incident board.

'Sally can you get me DI Barrow please?'

Chrissie was ready to brief the evening team. She waited for the call before heading in to explain what had happened and how they would investigate it.

'DI Barrow is on the line, putting him through.'

'Thanks Sally.'

Chrissie asked James to check any missing person's against the information and photographs they had discovered at the scene. The sooner they could identify the victim, the sooner they could investigate the circumstances leading up to the death. They would need as much information as possible. Anything at all that could lead to a possible motive was crucial right now.

She put all thoughts of Janny's special powers, what in her view was stupid mumbo jumbo, coincidental premonitions out of her mind, and went in to brief the evening shift before setting off to meet up with Janny.

*

The two women were sitting in the Ship Inn. They had ordered their meal and were sharing a bottle of white wine while they were waiting for their order to be served.

'You don't believe me do you? I think you'll find that what I said will come true. You won't be able to shrug that off will you?' Janny said as she toyed with her glass of wine.

'Bullshit.'

'OK if that's how you feel, fine.'

The conversation was beginning to get a bit heated. So the two women fell quiet. They ate and drank their wine in a relatively speechless state. They were both tired and they just wanted to unwind. Chrissie knew that Janny was going to have to perform the post-mortem in the morning and didn't want to antagonize her.

'Shall we go back to mine tonight? We can shower and get comfortable then just chill for the rest of the evening.' Chrissie suggested.

'Yeah, that sounds like a good plan.' A tired Janny whispered.

They went home showered, then they had a couple of glasses of wine, before making love. Then they retired to bed both weary from the day's events.

*

Mike and Sharon were back at Mike's place, they had been out earlier for their evening meal.

'The meal was lovely, I really enjoyed it Mike.' Sharon told him as she stripped out of her clothes.

'Fancy taking a shower with me before cracking open a bottle of plonk.' Mike suggested.

'Don't mind if I do my dear.' Sharon replied.

They showered while making mad passionate love, the water was cascading over their pulsating bodies. They were caressing each other in a soapy heaven. It was a lovely de-stressing end to another eventful day.

'Where's that plonk you promised me? You are definitely slipping, there was once a time you couldn't wait to get me hammered so you could have your wicked way with me. I should have made you wait until the drinks were flowing freely. I'm sure it would have come out much sooner.' Sharon joked.

'So sorry my lovely, you are right as usual. I should be more on the ball. Here darling, only the best for you my sweetheart.' Mike said as he passed her a drink.

They spent the rest of the evening watching a film on DVD. Then before retiring to bed, they caught up with the latest news.

Mike was feeling very content, his private life was wonderful at the moment. He didn't want that to ever go away. It was amazing how much his life had changed since he had met Sharon Trivett. Following his divorce, he had felt so down and depressed. Now all that had changed.

They watched as the newsreader informed the public of the body that had been discovered earlier that day. So victim number two was yet to be identified.'

After a short discussion about the latest murder, they had both agreed that it was going to be another tricky case. They were in for a busy day tomorrow. The couple finished off their wine and then made their way to bed. Following another raunchy and extremely rampant lovemaking session, they fell asleep in each other arms.

12

All Chrissie could do now was to wait for Janny's post- mortem findings. Once she had all the facts she could then try and determine what the motive might be. She might even be able to connect the killings if the murders turned out to be a similar match.

James, Mike and Sharon were busy following their own leads. James was almost certain that the missing persons list he had in front of him contained the identity of the unidentified body in the morgue. All he had to do was wait for the verifying information to confirm the link. He was secretly thankful that he didn't have all the responsibility that Chrissie had. Oh yes, it was great to be a Detective Chief Inspector. Brilliant as the status symbol would be, in all reality, he didn't think he could cope with the pressure a case like this would bring. No, definitely not a good place to be at this moment in time. He had the ambition and drive to hold down such a position but he knew deep down that it wasn't all it was cracked up to be.

James had gone through the list in front of him a few times. The last updated list had contained a few new names He continued to check out the missing person list to try an eliminate any that were not relevant to the case and concentrate on the ones that may be worth following up.

Mike and Sharon waded their way through the paperwork that had been gathered and collected since the second victim had turned up. So far the body hadn't been identified, so it was important that they check every possible avenue, to ensure that they didn't miss anything that could be vital in solving this case.

Janny had just finished the post-mortem examination on the second victim. She was horrified but not surprised to discover that this victim had also undergone heart surgery. He also had a puncture wound to his neck, the same as the other victim. Well, that confirmed her theory that this surgeon had been the same person that she had dreamed about. It was just confirming what she already knew.

This victim's heart had been removed like it had been in the first murder. The body was decomposing quickly but Janny knew she was right. This was the man she had dreamed about. Chrissie wouldn't like her referring to her dreams, but once his identity and profession has been revealed, she would have to believe her. Wouldn't she? It didn't really matter now what she thought. Janny knew she was right.

Janny asked her new assistant David Harris to finish off while she wrote a quick review of her findings for Chrissie. She sighed as she continued to write her review. She knew deep down that this was the person she had dreamed about. This would turn out to be the teacher. Surely Chrissie would have to admit that what she had told her about her dream was true. It was not the mumbo jumbo she believed it was at the moment.

13

Mary Smithe was sitting on her bed in her makeshift home. She had lit a cigarette and was listening to her portable radio. The voices had warned her not to make too much noise so she had the volume quite low. She listened to the news, which was all about another body being discovered. She shuddered as she inhaled on the cigarette.

The voices were now warning her of an impending danger. She was becoming very agitated, it wasn't fair. The safety of her new home had now become a far more dangerous place. Mary couldn't ignore the voices, they were always right. The noises she had thought she heard were probably more important than she had first thought. Someone else was also in this disused hospital, she didn't know who, or how the nature of their presence would impact on her stay here. All she knew was that her sanctuary was being threatened and because of this, she felt threatened too. It was important that she remained anonymous, she would have to find a weapon of some sort to protect herself if it became necessary.

Mary put out the cigarette in her makeshift kidney dish ashtray, then she set off to try and find something to protect herself with.

Slowly and quietly she looked through the old equipment that had been left there. She was hoping to find some scissors or an old discarded scalpel, there was nothing like that obviously on display at the moment. She continued to search the floor she was on.

There was no sign of anyone else on this floor. So provided she was very quiet and very careful she could stay there. At least for the time being. This was not fair, why can't she just stay here? She wasn't hurting anyone and she was very happy here. The voices agreed. Mary went back to her bed and lit another cigarette.

*

Stewart Colt had spent the last five years in prison. He had been convicted of various drug related crimes including dealing. He was not an addict himself, he wasn't that silly, he had made quite a lot of money selling drugs to weaker willed people. He had managed to stash away plenty of cash in lots of different locations so that it wouldn't be discovered and taken from him if he got caught. Now he was back on the streets so to speak, he would not have to worry about money.

Stewart Colt had recently discovered that he had a brother and a sister. They had all been taken into care as children and been separately adopted. He was both initially shocked and then excited to find his siblings. They were back together again as a family.

Stewart was saddened to learn that his brother was ill. His brother was five years younger than him. He had genuinely hoped that he and his sister could do something to help him. His sister had a few tricks up her sleeve, he would do whatever she wanted him to, in order to help to save their kid brother Alex

Wilson, who was twenty nine years old and had acute heart failure. Alex would definitely need a heart transplant at some stage and was already on the transplant waiting list. Now it had become a waiting game for the right donor to become available. Not ideal, but all he had if he was to survive. His condition was becoming rapidly worse, he would need to have a transplant soon or any hope of survival was lost.

Stewart had been very productive while he had been in Drayford Prison. He could have just bided his time, kept his nose clean and returned to his drug related crimes. Instead he had decided that he would utilise his time constructively. He studied lots of medical topics and decided on becoming a theatre nurse when he got out. He had shocked himself at how good he seemed to be at retaining information. He had finally gained enough knowledge to fulfil his ambition. Already proficient enough to start his medical training. He was very proud of his transition from being a drug dealer to becoming a theatre nurse. He was concentrating on heart transplant procedures. A very interesting and worthy profession. Stewart still had a way to go but because of his previous studies, he was well on the way to becoming a very good nurse.

Life was treating Stewart very good at the moment, he had served his time and would not be returning there in a hurry. Life held much more excitement outside the walls of a prison. He had his future career and a new found brother and sister to get to know. It was unfortunate he had been caught in the first place, but some good had come out of his stay in prison. Yes, he had everything going for him now. He just had to make sure he didn't spend too much of his ill-gotten gains so he didn't bring attention to himself. The last thing he wanted now would be to have the police snooping around wanting to know where all his money was coming from.

Stewart Colt was now officially a medical student and working on a placement in a private hospital that specialised in heart transplants. He also had a few other interests, but he would have to keep those to himself. It would only complicate matters, and that would never do. He had done well for himself, against all the odds. It had helped that his sister worked there too. She had put in a good word for him. Together they made a very good team.

*

Mary was listening to the radio, she was very worried about the recent discovery of a second body. She asked the voices what she should do. The voices told her not to panic but to stay alert. This was her home and she didn't want to leave here. She would do as the voices instructed. She would be careful and stay alert. She would be on a mega alert for any hostile activities happening here in this building.

*

Katherine Garfield was thirty one years old and a very proficient cardio vascular surgeon and consultant. She worked at the special heart unit, a private hospital in Drayfield. She had visited the Lockington Royal Infirmary on many occasions to give lectures in heart surgery to students. Sometimes she was asked if she would assist the heart surgeons that worked there. She had met Dr Janny Stowers on quite a few occasions during her visits. Katherine knew that Dr Stowers was one of the best heart surgeons in the country. She knew that Janny was also a medical examiner and that she worked in forensic science to assist the police in any suspicious deaths or murder cases. Katherine liked and respected Janny.

The telephone rang in Katherine's office, it was Dr Stowers' assistant David Harris. He had called to ask her if she would be able to cover for Dr Stowers while she was out on her police and forensic business. Katherine said she would be able to cover a few hours if that was ok. David said that would help immensely during Janny's absence.

David informed Janny that Dr Katherine Garfield would be able to cover for a few hours while she was away.

'That's brilliant David, thanks for arranging that for me.'

'No problem, is there anything you would like me to do?'

Janny thought for a moment and said it would be very helpful if he could liaise with the lab to try and get the tox results through. He could go over to the lab and use his charm on the team. Maybe his presence would speed things up a bit.

'If you happen to get any results, could you let me and DCI Charles know a.s.a.p.'

'Of course I will Dr Stowers, glad to be of help.'

'Thank you David, that's great. I'd like to concentrate on my autopsy report for DCI Charles. So that will help me no end. If you're back when Dr Garfield arrives, could you brief her on my patient caseload for today? If you're not there don't worry I've left my schedule for her. If she can only do a few hours, she can concentrate on the more urgent cases. I'll take care of the rest when I get back later.'

Janny rang Chrissie and informed her of the missing heart.

'It means that we have a serial killer out there. I would say from the evidence I've seen so far, this is definitely the same killer. I'm going to write out your report, then I'm going to get a bit of lunch before going back to the hospital. David, my new assistant is being very helpful, he certainly is an asset. It leaves me free to concentrate on my reports and other things that I need to do. Shall we meet up for lunch?'

'Sorry Janny, I can't make it for lunch, I've got too much on here. Let's meet up after work in the pub. Will that be ok for you?'

'Yes Chrissie, that will be lovely darling, text me later to let me know where we are going and what time.'
'I will. Can you fax me the autopsy report through when you've completed it, and any results from the lab? I've got another meeting with Cheryl soon, so I'm going to grab a bite to eat now.'

'Ok, I'll speak to again soon, don't work too hard.'

When she had finished the call, Janny set off to the café to get something to eat. She hadn't realised just how hungry she was. Her stomach was rumbling, she was starving.

Janny sat in Jack's café, she had ordered a coffee and a BLT sandwich. She was lost in her own thoughts when she noticed someone approaching. It was the new police constable Amy Campbell.

'Hi Janny, I'm on my lunch break, is it ok if I join you?' Amy asked as she pulled out the seat and sat opposite.

Janny made a mental note to herself. She must let Chrissie know about this crush or whatever it was that Amy had on her. It wasn't healthy for either of them, especially now that Chrissie was suddenly turning into a jealous person. She'd never shown any jealous tendencies before. There were a lot of things that had changed recently. It seemed to be that a lot of niggly things were pissing them both off. Janny didn't want anything to happen to their relationship. They had always been so good together, she didn't want to lose the rapport they had shared over the last eighteen years. It was too much of a coincidence that Amy always seemed to be bumping into her and it was getting more and more frequent. It felt like she was being stalked and who knows, maybe she was.

Following a text message to confirm the time and the place, Chrissie and Janny set off to meet each other for a well-deserved evening meal.

The two women met up in the Ship Inn and had a glass of wine and a meal. They ate in a cosy corner of the pub in silence. Janny attempted to tell Chrissie about her suspicions of Amy her new recruit.

'Bullshit, are you sure you aren't imagining it or instigating it in some way?'

'Chrissie, I'm only telling you this to reassure you that if you see anything untoward it's a crush thing and not me that's interested in any way, shape or form.'

'Okay, I'll have a word with Amy, she needs taking down a peg or two anyway.'

The atmosphere was a bit uncomfortable for a while. Soon though, as they drank their second glass of wine, the rest of the night beckoned. They were both beginning to unwind and relax. Both the women were looking forward to going home together and doing what they always enjoyed together. The conversation went from the murder investigation to the relaxing evening they both craved.

*

Back home later that evening.

'Chrissie, if you play your cards right, I think I'll try and find your G. spot tonight.' Janny said as she grinned.

'It's in my knicker drawer.' Chrissie told her.

'What is? Oh you silly sod.'

'My G thingy, it's in with my knickers.'

'No, not your G string, your G spot. I hope that isn't in your knicker drawer.' Janny chuckled.

'No, only joking. Ok then, you'd better get your finger out and find my G string…. Oops, Sorry, I meant G spot.' Chrissie smiled as she made her way to the kitchen.

'I wonder if you'll find the G thingy in here.'

Janny smiled as she helped Chrissie onto the kitchen work surface.

'Well I'd better have a look then, as long as it isn't in your knicker drawer. I have a feeling I'll find it up here somewhere.' Janny said as she proceeded to look for the missing G spot.

'Actually, it should be the other way round, you should be looking for my G spot. You are the DCI.'

'Ohhh, noooo, its ok you can keep looking …… Ohhh, I think you've found it. Oh yes, that's definitely the missing G thingy…… oooooooooh yyyyyyyeeeesssss…..' Chrissie screamed.

'Well I think I found your G spot.'

'Good God Janny, you did, you found it, eureka.'

The girls continued to cuddle and caress each other for a while, it was as lovely as always. They both knew how to please each other. They finished the bottle of wine and watched a bit of TV before going to bed.

During the night Janny had another one of her special dreams. In her dream she had witnessed another murder. Janny knew that she would have to tell Chrissie just in case it was important in her investigation. Chrissie wouldn't be happy about it, but she had to try and help if she could.

The dream showed her that the next victim would be an electrician. His body would be found minus his heart in a field near Hairdale common. She had seen the surgeon but not his face. It was always covered in a surgical mask and he was always in scrubs.

14

Chrissie answered her phone, it was DI Barrow.

'DCI Chrissie Charles.'

'I've found out the identity of the second victim, it's David Blackstock. A Teacher aged 27. Separated from his wife Emma Blackstock, moved back in with his parents after the separation. He was reported missing by his parents when he didn't return home after school.'

Chrissie thanked DI James Barrow and ended the call. Then reality set in. Janny would have bet money on the victim being a teacher. She had seen it in her weird dreams. This time Chrissie knew she couldn't very well shrug this off as hocus pocus. Her instincts said don't go there, but deep down she knew this was much more than she had ever anticipated. This seemed so unreal, and yet it was becoming very real. It unnerved Chrissie, it went against everything she believed in, but the truth was, she couldn't deny or ignore the fact that Janny was right.

Chrissie was feeling very hot, the weather was oppressive and it was making it hard to breathe. She freshened herself up as best she could, then she set out with the team to do a little hands on work. The door to door enquiries hadn't revealed much. They were in the process of interviewing the parents of the teacher. Following that they would interview his estranged wife. Chrissie wished it would cool down a bit outside. She was feeling very hot and bothered at the moment.

Outside the weather was changing, the sky had suddenly darkened. Black clouds had appeared where the sun had previously been shining. There was an eerie silence as the atmosphere became very quiet and still. A thunder storm was rapidly approaching, it looked as though they were in for a heavy downpour. In the distance, the sound of the thunder was getting ever closer.

Janny could see the lightening from the window in her office. A loud clap of thunder made her jump.

'Shit.' She said aloud as the thunder rattled around the hospital.

It was time for her break, Janny was about to go out for lunch. She soon changed her mind and decided to stay in the hospital and catch up on her work there. She would have something to eat in the canteen first.

Chrissie rang to let her know she was out interviewing people who had known David Blackstock. They had arranged to meet after work. Chrissie was reluctantly beginning to accept Janny's premonitions.

Janny's mother Rose rang, to ask if she would be going to Marie's birthday party at the weekend. Her niece would be turning thirteen, the party was to be held on the Saturday at her sister Denise's house. She told her mum that she would be there if she could. Janny and her niece were very close and she always looked forward to seeing her. She'd have a word with Chrissie tonight to see if it would be possible for them to take a few hours out on Saturday to be there at the party.

Torrential rain was pounding the steamy pavements, bouncing back up with the momentum of the storm. The temperature had dropped a few degrees, which now made life a little more tolerable. Chrissie was grateful for that.

She had spent the afternoon interviewing, she'd also completed some paperwork. Gradually she had ruled out any friends and family during the earlier interviews. It had been confirmed, they had a serial killer at large. She would have to use all the appropriate systems, procedures and resources she had at her disposal during the investigation nothing could be left to chance.

Later that evening.

The two women were dining in the Traveller's Rest. It had been a long day for both of them. The music was soft and soothing, it had a calming effect. Janny ordered a sirloin steak cooked medium rare with fries. Chrissie had opted for the hunters chicken. They shared a bottle of wine as they began to unwind.

'Do you think we'll be able to pop over to my sisters on Saturday for a couple hours? I'd like to be there at Marie's birthday bash. We don't have to stay too long, I know you want to be nearby in case anything evolves in the murder investigation.'

'Yes, I think it'll do us both good to have a break from things here for a while.' Chrissie told her as she downed the rest of her wine.

'I'm ready to go if you are, it's been a long day, and we need a bit of down time to unwind a bit. We've got a few hours left before bedtime, so let's chill at mine tonight.' Janny suggested.

'That sounds like a plan.' Chrissie agreed.

They showered and changed, then opened another bottle of wine. The night was still relatively young, it would be nice to chill and of course make love, they had both agreed on that plan.

'Will you believe me when I tell you about my dreams now?' Janny asked as she kissed Chrissie's neck.

'Ohhhh, you don't half pick your moments to ask me shit.'

'Well do you?' Janny asked as she worked her way down Chrissie's body.

'Ok, I believe you! Now can you get on with the job in hand please darling...... ohhhhhh, yes that's it, that's good, oh fuck…. That's it…. Oh yyyyyeessssss.'

Later that evening.

'I've had another special dream.' Janny told Chrissie. 'It was about another victim who I believe to be an electrician. His body was left in a field near Hairdale common. I saw the surgeon like in the other dreams, but he always has his scrubs on and his face covered.'

'I hope you're wrong Janny, I really hope your wrong this time.'

Janny knew she wasn't wrong but didn't say anything. They would soon find out when they found the body.

*

Neil Jordon had just finished his last visit for the day. It hadn't been too bad. He was looking forward to getting home to his wife and new baby. His wife Catherine had given birth to their first child Seb just three weeks ago. Neil was so proud of his wife and son. Life is so much more worth living now, it couldn't get much better than this he thought. He was totally thankful and very happy.

Feeling blessed, Neil got into his work van. He sent a text to his wife Cathy to let her know he was on his way home as usual. He offered to call in for a take away on his way back. Cathy sent a text back, saying that would be great.

Neil stopped off at a chip shop just outside Hairdale and ordered fish and chips for them both. Then he made his way home. He glanced at his rear view mirror and noticed a Range rover speeding towards him.

'Wanker.' He thought. 'Some people shouldn't

be allowed on the roads.'

He moved closer to the edge of the country lane to allow the idiot to overtake him.

The Range rover passed Neil's vehicle at speed. As it did so, it cut in front of his van causing him to slam on the breaks to slow down. The Range rover then slowed down and positioned the vehicle so that Neil had to stop.

'This is ridiculous, the driver must be a nutcase.' Neil thought angrily.

Neil Jordan stopped his van and before he had time to react, the person who had been driving the Range rover stabbed the needle into his neck through the open window. He felt a sharp stabbing pain in his neck as the needle pierced his skin.

The next thing Neil knew, was the realisation that he was strapped to a table with a bright light shining down on him. Slowly the reality of what was happening was becoming all too clear.

The surgeon loomed over Neil.

'This can't be happening. It's got to be a bad dream, he would wake up soon, wouldn't he?' Neil hoped as a deep black darkness took over his last rational thoughts.

*

Three weeks later.

Another body had been discovered in a field near Hairdale Common. Chrissie was called to the scene.

Janny met up with her there. James and Mike had arrived there first following the call in.

The first response team had cordoned of the area where the body had been discovered. The team had created a log, noting everyone who had crossed the barrier since the scene had been secured. Anyone who crossed the barrier now would have to wear protective clothing. The one piece cover all suits, foot covers, latex gloves, and face masks etc.

They would all have to be collected and bagged before the users left the scene. This was to avoid any risk of losing any trace evidence. During a systematic search for evidence a leading investigator will assign individuals to a particular area while the scene is processed. The investigator will be overlooking the search and the collection of evidence.

Before anything is moved or touched, the entire initial area must be processed and fully documented, to ensure that a permanent record exists of the scene. This is to record the condition in which any evidence was found and to document who had collected it. The timeline and description of any items collected, along with any general notes of the scene will also be recorded. Extensive photographic reference is also important in all areas of the crime scene.

Once the documentation of the scene is complete, the crime officers can proceed to collect physical evidence. The body is inspected by the forensic pathologist. Sometimes the hands and feet are covered with plastic bags to prevent the loss of trace evidence.

'How's it going' Chrissie asked the forensic team.

Andrew MacDonald one of the forensic team investigators, informed Chrissie what they had done and collected so far. He brought her up to speed with where they were at so far.

Janny went over to Chrissie.

'David, my new assistant is here, as part of his training, to gain some experience in hands on work. He seems to be doing fine, I'm very pleased with his progress.' Janny told her.

'Glad to hear it Janny, I hope he is being highly supervised with it being a murder investigation. We don't want any forensic cock up's do we?'

'Of course, that goes without saying. Anyway I know this body will turn out to be someone I have dreamed about recently. I've been able to work out so far from the dream, that this man could be an electrician. I have a strong feeling that he is a family man, he probably has a new baby and a wife. These thoughts came to me while I was asleep or whatever state it was. If I think of anything else I'll let you know. Once the post-mortem has been done I'll let you have the results.'

'Hmm, thanks Janny.' Chrissie automatically cringed at the mention of the dreams. She knew it was strange but she couldn't ignore them totally, just in case they were important in some way to her investigation.

*

DI Barrow and DS Hartley were assigned to the case along with a team of officers. DS Trivett was assigned to the missing person side of things. This done, DCI Chrissie Charles rounded up the briefing.

'Good Luck' Chrissie told them. 'I think we're going to need it.'

Chrissie went into an arranged meeting with Cheryl Teal. The Criminal Psychologist had brought a criminal profile for Chrissie.

'I've got the profile report here for you. I'll just run through it quickly with you. I know you are busy so I won't take up too much of your time.'

'Thanks Cheryl, I hope you can shed some light on this surgeon person. This is the third victim now, I don't want to have this killer free to carry on regardless. I just don't know much at the moment. We're waiting for the toxicology reports and DNA sample results which takes time. In the meantime, any help you can give me in the profile would be really helpful.'

Sally sauntered into the meeting room with her usual tray of hot coffees and an assortment of biscuits. Both the women thanked her as she placed the tray on the desk between them.

'Well, in my report, I've pointed out a few options. These are based on the information we have about the killer at the moment.'

'Anything you have will be a plus Cheryl.' Chrissie said as she took a sip of her coffee.

'It could be someone who broke the surgeon's heart that triggered the murders. It could be a psychotic episode of a mentally ill patient. Or it could be someone who is medically trained and was let down in some way or other. It could be a surgeon who had a malpractice conviction and was struck off. It could be a medically trained person who has someone close to them who is in need of a heart transplant and the waiting list isn't an option anymore. Or it could be a medically trained person who has suffered some sort of breakdown. The person could have come from an unstable background and had medical training.' Cheryl told Chrissie.

Cheryl stopped for a moment to get her breath and have a sip of her coffee.

'It could be someone with enough power and influence to organise the kidnappings and the ensuing operations. Whoever did the operations must have had an accomplice, someone to help in some way. I can't see anyone able to do this alone. I may be wrong but I don't think so.'

'I agree with that Cheryl, one person would find it very difficult. I don't know about the motive, it could be any one of the options you've suggested. I'll get someone to investigate the sort of people that could have had the motive and expertise. Thanks for that, it gives me an idea of the type of people I should be looking for. I just don't know where to look yet but I will. My first job is to check out any known criminals that would be in a position to organise it.'

'Another option is, it could be something to do with body part trafficking or something on those lines.'

Cheryl said as she finished off her coffee.

'I'll do another updated profile as soon as I get more info. Good luck with the investigation Chrissie. I know this must be hard for you and Janny after what happened in your last investigation.'

'Thanks Cheryl. I am a bit worried about Janny though. Ever since the last murder case and her near death experience she has been having strange dreams. She says that she see's things to do with the murders we are investigating at the moment. I didn't believe her at first, but she was convinced that the dreams were some sort of premonition. Now I've found that there's some truth in what she has dreamed. I don't know what to believe right now. I would much prefer to do this by the scientific evidence rather than the supernatural approach. I still find it very hard to accept that it is anything other than coincidence. But she has been right on quite a lot of the facts that we didn't know about until much later.'

'There have been many NDE (near death experience) patients who have found themselves outside of their bodies observing details that were happening far away. This is called Veridical

Perception and it is currently unexplainable by modern science. NDE's can happen to people of all races, genders, education, marital status and social class. Drugs are not a factor. NDE's are not hallucinations. People tend to lose their fear of death and appreciate life more following a near death experience. People's lives are transformed. British scientists have announced that there is convincing evidence that people who have had a near death experience are capable of paranormal feats. Such as premonitions, telepathy, and out of body experiences. This is also known as a sixth sense. The same things have been reported around the world and it can affect both children and adults.' Cheryl explained.

'I had no idea. Thanks for explaining, and thanks for the profile Cheryl, much appreciated.'

'No problem, I'll be in touch again when I get more info.' Cheryl told her as she made her way out.

15

Janny had noticed that she was bumping into Amy Campbell quite often now. It really was as though she was stalking her.

'It's got to be in my imagination.' Janny thought. *'Amy is a fit young woman, she wouldn't be interested in an old goat like me…. Would she?'*

As Janny entered the police headquarters, there Amy was again. She was smiling and staring at her. Janny felt uncomfortable. She would definitely have to have a word with Chrissie again, as soon as she had the chance to bring the subject up.

In the incident room, Chrissie was busy briefing her team. Janny went into the major incident room and sat down to listen to what Chrissie had to say. She noticed that Amy had followed her into the room.

Chrissie looked up as Janny walked in, she also noticed Amy Campbell follow her in. She thought it was strange that every time Janny was at the station, Amy wasn't far behind her. Was Amy stalking Janny? She didn't know what to think or what to believe.

DI James Barrow had moved to the front of the incident room to where the white boards were. He pointed to the pictures of the latest victim. James had some information on this person and he began to inform the team.

'The missing person investigations, DS Hartley and DS Trivett have been following up have provided us with the identity of the third victim. His name is Neil Jordan. He is an electrician and is married with a baby, three weeks old.'

Chrissie cringed slightly when James mentioned that the victim was an electrician. She remembered what Janny had told her. That the next victim would be an electrician. Janny was right yet again, she couldn't deny that. Then like a bolt of lightning Chrissie realised that Janny ticked all the boxes.

'Why didn't I think of that before? Janny has the knowledge and she knows far too much about the murders not to have had some sort of involvement in these heartless murders.' Chrissie thought.

Janny had suddenly become a prime suspect in the murder investigation. She had the expertise and influence to perform the operations. Janny had made herself a suspect by admitting that she knew things about the victims that only the killer would have known.

Chrissie decided to keep this information to herself for now. There was no need to inform Janny yet, but if anything else came to light she would have to seriously consider taking Janny off the case pending a formal investigation. They would need to look into her whereabouts at the time and places of the three victims.

'What the hell am I thinking here? I'm actually

considering accusing my partner of three serial murders. Am I that desperate to find the killer? I've lived with Janny all these years and I know she wouldn't hurt a fly never mind kill three people. I must be cracking up.' She thought to herself.

Chrissie's instincts as a DCI were pointing her towards Janny though. How was she supposed to ignore this? She couldn't.

16

Chrissie looked across the room to where Janny was, Amy Campbell was sitting right behind her. She'd noticed that Amy was paying Janny a lot of attention lately. It might all be in her mind but she didn't think so. Amy was always close by when Janny visited the station.

Janny caught Chrissie's attention and smiled across at her. Chrissie's response was quite cool. She half-heartedly smiled back at Janny, but her eyes were devoid of feeling.

Chrissie had put together a list of potential suspects. The worrying thing about it was, that Janny had become her prime suspect. Oh how she wished she could turn back time. To go back to the place they were in before the stamp master had taken over their lives. '

That's never going to happen, so it's got to be onwards and upwards, there is no going back.' She thought.

*

'Don't forget we're going to Denise's tomorrow afternoon if that's still ok. I've managed to get Marie a birthday present and card. My mum will be there too and I haven't seen her in ages. It will be nice to catch up on all the family gossip.' Janny told Chrissie.

'Yes, its fine, I think we could do with a bit of a breather from the case.'

They spent the evening drinking wine and watching TV. Janny was becoming very apprehensive about the murder cases. She had a feeling there was more to come. She was dreading the accompanying dreams that came with them.

The following morning they called in at the station to check for any updates since last night. Nothing had been reported. The night duty sergeant was getting ready to leave, he was waiting to handover to the daytime staff. Following a quick chat with him, the two women left and got into Janny's ford focus.

They set off to go and see Janny's niece Marie. It was hard to believe that Marie was thirteen today. It didn't seem that long ago Janny was bouncing her up and down on her knee. Time is flying by at a frightening rate.

Marie's birthday party went very well and both Janny and Chrissie enjoyed it. It was a welcome break from the hassle of the murder cases. They'd both been relaxed and happy whilst at Janny's sister's house. It was something they both needed at the moment. Deep down though, Chrissie was still pondering on the case she was under so much pressure to solve. They left the party in the early evening after saying their goodbyes. It had done them both the world of good to get away from everything, even if it was only for a short time.

When the two women arrived home, they'd remained in a happy mood. After freshening up, they laughed and joked with each other. Then the night progressed into an evening of wonderful sex, washed down with a bottle of red wine to finish off the day with style.

*

The following morning.

It was a lovely sunny morning with a warmth that was promising a very hot day to come. It was lovely outside at the moment. It wasn't too hot, just warm enough to be comfortable before the searing heat kicked in. The slight breeze made it easier to breathe, the humidity was lower this morning. Ideal conditions for a nice comfortable breakfast before having to face the long day ahead of them.

'Yesterday was brilliant.' Janny told Chrissie.

'Yes, I really enjoyed it too.' Chrissie replied. 'Today's breakfast my darling is my new concoction. I have called it poached on toast. I may put it in my recipe book when I write it. Poached eggs on a slice of buttered toast, simple but wholesome food don't you think?'

'Yeah, fine.' Janny told her as she sipped the coffee Chrissie had put in front of her.

'Well at least it looks better than that scrambled omelette concoction that you created. That was a horrible mess.'

'What are you saying?'

'Nothing, this poached on toast isn't bad, tastes nice and looks a lot better than that scrambled shit you served before.'

The two women ate breakfast and drank coffee until they were both contented enough to face the day.

*

Lunchtime

Janny met up with Chrissie at the station for lunch. She'd brought them a sandwich each and a small cake, then put them on Chrissie's desk while she went to the loo.

While she was heading back from the toilet, Janny came across Amy Campbell. Amy headed straight for Janny and she intercepted her. She looked Janny straight in the eyes and lunged forward steeling a kiss. Janny was so shocked, that for a moment, it took a little while for her to realise what was happening. The kiss went on for much longer than it should have because of Janny's slight hesitation due to the shock.

A split second after Amy had launched the kiss, Chrissie came out of her office. She saw Janny and Amy kissing full on, and a fire raged inside her like she had never known or felt before. She went back inside her office and briefly watched from the open door.

What the hell? This can't be happening, Janny and Amy, no way, surely not. I must be seeing things. Here in the

station in front of everyone who happens to see this. No way, why would Janny do this to me….. The bloody bitch.'
Chrissie thought as she retreated back inside her office and closed the door.

Janny pulled away from Amy.

'What the hell are you playing at Amy, why are you doing this? I hope for your sake you have a good explanation. This kind of behaviour is inexcusable and will not be tolerated or accepted. It's a form of harassment and stalking. It's totally unacceptable and unforgivable anywhere, never mind here in the work place. I'll be speaking with DCI Charles about this. So you have been warned.'
'I'm so sorry Dr Stowers, I don't know what came over me, please forgive me.' Amy said with tears in her eyes as she ran off and out of the station.'

Janny couldn't believe what had just happened.

When Janny went back into Chrissie's office and closed the door all hell broke loose.'

'What the fuck are you up to with Amy? I saw the two of you kissing, in here of all places, not hiding it from anyone who happened to be passing. You bitch, after all these years you have decided to go with someone else and you're not even bothered to be discreet about it. I can't believe what I've just seen. I wouldn't have imagined that happening in a million years. Why would you do this to me, why?'

'Chrissie, let me explain what happened, it's not

what you think at all. Not in any shape or form. Nothing is going on between us and never will.'

'Go fuck yourself. I know what I saw, you are a bloody cradle snatcher and a liar. You should be ashamed of yourself, you bitch.'

'Don't be silly, you know I wouldn't do that. Amy has a stupid crush on me. I have no idea why, it was she who came to me and planted that kiss. I was so taken aback, that for a moment, I didn't know what was happening. As soon as I realised, I broke away from her, she has left the station crying.'

'She'll bloody cry when I've done with her, she's messing with the wrong DCI. I'm going to transfer her with a vengeance. She won't know what's bloody hit her, the tarty bitch. She'll regret the day she crossed me, I swear she will. And you can get the hell out of my sight, I know what I saw and you were a big part of it. It takes two to tango, how could you do this to me and then try to deny it?'

'Chrissie please, I didn't kiss her, she came on to me. I pushed her away as soon as I realised what was happening. It all happened so quickly, I wasn't expecting it, please believe me.'

'Go fuck yourself, you tarty lying bitch.'

'Chrissie please believe me, you must know deep down that I would never do that to you. You know that I wouldn't hurt you like that. We've been so good together all these years, why would I ever want to spoil that? It's not what it seemed, you only saw the action and not what happened afterwards. Amy has been more or less stalking me for a while. I was beginning to get unnerved about it all. I did try to tell you, and I meant to tell you about all my fears. Then this murder case came along and I didn't have the chance to bring it up again. I didn't want to worry you about something that might have been trivial and probably all in my imagination. I didn't expect the kiss, please believe me.'

'I don't know what to believe right now. At one time, I would never have given it much credence, I know you better than that. But recently I've noticed that we are having some problems in our relationship. We've gradually been drifting apart. We're both guilty of brushing everything under the carpet. Pretending that nothing has altered, knowing everything has changed. I know what I saw.'

'I told you what happened.'

'We really need a break from each other. After what you have done it is a certainty. There's no way I'm going home with you tonight. Don't bother calling round to mine because I don't want you there. I don't want you anywhere near me, so get the hell out of my sight.'

'Please Chrissie.'

'Piss off.' Don't bother coming to mine tonight I can't stand the sight of you.'

'Come on Chrissie, you don't have to do this. Nothing has happened. Nothing at all.'

'There's no smoke without fire. We'll obviously have to see each other in the course of our work, but that's it. I don't want to see you in any other capacity.' Chrissie told her.

Janny knew there was nothing more she could do. Chrissie refused to believe her. She reluctantly retreated from the office clutching the sandwich she was going to have for lunch.

Chrissie couldn't settle now knowing that things had come to a head between them. She felt so sad and down.

Why did this have to happen when they had so much work on at the moment? It wasn't helping one little bit.'

Chrissie was going to have this out with Amy. It was eating away at her.

Janny had also become her prime suspect in the heartless murders. Everything was becoming surreal, this wasn't in any way natural.

'How the hell had Janny become a murder suspect?' Chrissie thought. *'Janny had made herself a prime suspect because she knows things about the murders. This was all brought about because of her so called premonitions. I'm going to have to take her off the case and out of the investigation until her name is cleared. I have to, it's my job. I can't ignore anything that may be relevant to the case.'*

Chrissie sent Janny an email.

'Dear Janny,

I'm not in a position to ignore the fact that you have now become a prime suspect in the murder investigation. I wouldn't be doing my job properly if I didn't follow up on all the clues. I have to go through the process to rule out anything that could place you inside the murder scene. You will need some solid alibis for the dates the victims went missing and murdered. You must understand that this is because you've apparently had inside information that only the killer would have known. It places me in a very difficult situation here. You also have the knowledge and expertise to carry out the operations that were performed on the victims. I'm sorry Janny but that's how it is. I'm not sure that I know you anymore. You are definitely not the woman I once knew. I have always trusted you and up until the time you nearly died, I would have given my life for you without hesitation. But now, I really don't know how I feel. It's very important that we keep our distance until things are resolved one way or another.

Sorry to have to say this. But I can't hide this from the investigation.

Chris x'

She sent the message.

*

Janny couldn't believe her eyes when she read Chrissie's message. How could she even contemplate her being involved with the murders? How could she? Her mind ran riot trying to put everything that had happened into perspective.

Janny sent Chrissie a reply.

Chrissie,

You cannot possibly imagine how hurt I feel. I can't believe what I have just read. It's so unfair and I don't know what to do about it. I've tried to explain to you everything about what happened between Amy, and myself which was bugger all. My premonitions are real, I had another one last night and was going to tell you about it later but what the hell. I saw a young woman I think she may have been a prostitute. She had blond hair and I saw a man rape her and then stab her in the chest. It appeared to be in a vehicle. I don't think this is the work of the Heartless killer. This could be another killer at large, if so god help us. I didn't kill her either, just in case you was going to put me at the top of your suspect list when you discover the body. The body appeared to have been dumped from the vehicle into a road. I'm not sure where the body is but it will be turning up shortly I'm convinced of that.'

'I hope you can find it in your heart to believe me, but whatever I say to you I can't convince you can I? Good luck with the investigations. I'm here if you need me in a professional capacity.

Your very upset and disappointed Janny.'

Chrissie read the reply to her message and tears fell down her face as she fought hard to control them.

*

James and Mike had been following up leads on the missing person list. So far they had a few people of interest.

Chrissie had the list in front of her.

Missing person list….

Mary Smithe….Escaped from an acute psychiatric ward.

Gabby Fielding….   A nurse.

Alan Denning….   Victim number one.

David Blackstock….   Victim number two.

Neil Jordan ….   Victim number three.

Terry Callum ….   Missing not yet accounted for.

Jane Stevens ….   Missing not yet accounted for.

Tanya Colleen ….   Missing not yet accounted for.

Pippa Downing …. Missing not yet accounted for.

These were within the timescale they had been looking in.

Chrissie had scribbled a list of people she thought could have been involved in the murders.

Suspects.

Mary Smithe ….Escaped from a psychiatric ward.

David Harris….Janny's new Assistant.

Amy Campbell….Chrissie's new recruit.

And right at the top of the list went…

Dr Janny Stowers Chrissie's partner.

'Not a lot to go on. Oh well, it's a start.' Chrissie thought to herself.

She would look into this later.

Chrissie decided that it would be a good idea to go out with her team to try and gain some insight into what was happening in the investigations. The rest of the day she was out and about. Questions were asked and replies were essential.

17

Jane Stevens was tired, she had been busy with her clients all night. It was time to go home. Her home was a big house divided into bedsits. Her bedsit was her home, she always tried to keep it relatively clean. Her drug habit had interfered with life somewhat, but on the whole she was managing her control her life quite successfully between her fixes. The pimp she was working for always took a large amount of her earnings before she got her own cut. To be fair though, the bedsit was free and the regular supply of crack was just enough to take the edge off and keep her fixed. This helped her to stay in control, so that she didn't lose her faculties completely. These were very good perks of the job. Her health had obviously suffered somewhat, but things could have been a hell of a lot worse. She was very lucky really and she knew it.

Jane was on her way home when someone in a black range rover come up alongside her.

'You up for it babe?' The man said to her.

'I'm just on my way home lovey.' Jane told him.

'I'll make it worth your while.'

Jane thought about it quickly and decided that one last punter might just provide enough extra money to pay for a lovely new dress she had seen recently, it had caught her eye. She would look very nice in it.

'Ok lovey, let's go for it, can we do the business in your car?'

'Of course, no problem, get in.' He ushered her into the car. Once he had settled himself into the driver's seat he triggered the central locking and Jane had now become his captive.'

'Don't say a word. I'm going to rape you beat you to a pulp and then I'm going to kill you. Now, how do you feel about that my dear?'

Jane thought he was enacting a fantasy scenario. She was used to the many weird and wonderful sexual fantasies with some of her clients. She soon found out that this was no game, this was for real.

'Hey, come on lovey, don't try to frighten me. I've had much worse than you love.'

The man laughed at her and smiled.

'I really don't think so.'

Jane was beginning to feel uneasy, was this man really going to hurt her? Jane tried the car door but it wouldn't open. She tried to scream as he pounced onto her and began to grope her body. It was then that she realised he really was going to force himself upon her. This was not looking good. The man hit her full in the face splitting her lips with the full force of his brute strength. The scream had frozen in Jane's throat when he had punched her in the face. He repeatedly hit her until she had lost all her energy to fight back. Jane knew that if she didn't fight him back now, she would almost certainly die here. She would need all her strength to fight back and hers was all but depleted now.

'Listen lovey.' Jane mumbled through her swollen bloody lips. 'You don't have to do this. I'll do whatever you want me to do and of course it will be all free of charge.'

'Shut up bitch.' He said as he punched her in the stomach knocking all the breath out of her.

He fumbled clumsily with her scanty underwear then he forced his large penis deep inside her. Jane couldn't do anything to save herself. She was completely at his mercy, this nightmare was real and there was no way of getting out of it. Her mind wandered as he raped her, she thought about her past, her present and the fact that she was going to be minus a future. Jane felt a deep feeling of hopelessness overcome her, she felt very sad.

She had resigned to the fact that this living hell of a nightmare was the harsh beginning of the end of her life. He was doing some horrendous things to her as he continued to rape her. Her life was about to be terminated and brought to an abrupt end by whoever this man was. Who was he? And why had he picked on her? She had never seen him before. She tried unsuccessfully to fight off her attacker, it was impossible to escape from him. The man continued to brutalise and abuse her battered body. He forced her down deeper into the reclined seat as he continued to torture her helpless body.

Jane hardly felt the sharpness of the knife as it sunk deep into her heart. The world that Jane Stevens had known and lived for the last twenty five years had come to an abrupt end. As the darkness pulled her closer to death, Jane ceased to exist. From that moment on she was just another statistic, another murder to solve. Jane Stevens didn't exist anymore. Her life had been cruelly taken from her. Jane could see a bright light getting increasingly closer, it comforted her and gave her a feeling of peace. At last she was free from the pain and suffering. She was uplifted to a much better place than the one she had once lived in. Jane Stevens was dead.

18

The surgeon was deliberating as to when the last attempt at a transplant would take place. This would be the final attempt, if this one didn't work it was game over. The time was running away so quickly, and the freedom of being undetected was getting less. The surgeon had recently noticed that they had acquired a squatter. The woman living on the floor below was becoming more curious, it wouldn't be long before she started to explore and maybe stumble into the operating theatre. That would leave no other option but to kill her. As long as she kept herself to herself she wouldn't be a problem. If she became too curious then she could become a real threat.

The squatter seemed to be in her own little world doing her own thing and not interfering in what the surgeon was doing, no doubt at some point this would change. That along with the fact the police were getting ever closer. There wasn't that much time left, it would become more risky as each day passed.

The nurse that had been held prisoner to assist the surgeon was trying to think of ways to escape. Gabby Fielding was a trained nurse so the wellbeing of her patients came natural to her. She had put this into practice when she was assisting the surgeon and the assistant she had with her during the heart operations. She didn't know what was going on but it obviously wasn't legal. Keeping her here against her will wasn't legal either. As if that wasn't bad enough, she also had to endure the torturous sex attacks. Gabby hated that the most, she would love to get her own back. If she could get hold of a scalpel she would cut off his dick and feed it to him.

Gabby knew she had to get out of her prison while she still could. She had a profound feeling of foreboding that things were maybe coming to the end. If that was the case then her days may be numbered. She wondered if the surgeon was dealing with transplant hearts for patients who either didn't meet the criteria for the transplant list or they were too ill to wait any longer for a new heart. Whatever the reasons for the transplants may be, Gabby knew that it was only a matter of time before the surgeon didn't need her anymore. When that time arrived she would be surplus to requirements and would probably be killed.

Stuart Colt donned an operating theatre gown and scrubbed up. He was looking forward to seeing the nurse again he fancied her like mad, but he wasn't allowed to go near her. He had to obey the surgeon's wishes, so for now he would get his kicks in a different way.

He was proud to have actually taken part in the heart transplant operations. He was grateful that his sister had pulled a few strings and he was working a few days a week assisting in operations in the private hospital where she worked. He had a lot to thank her for. He didn't want her to find out what he had been getting up to in his free time. Stuart knew that she wouldn't approve.

Anything was better than being in Drayford prison.

19

Chrissie was upset and still very angry, she didn't want to see either Amy or Janny at this point in time.

Amy was feeling very guilty since she had kissed Janny. She would have to come clean about it. Chrissie had laced into Janny, Amy had heard some shouting as she silently crept back into the station. Amy had then gone straight into the loo sobbing her heart out. This had turned out to be a total disaster. Amy had been infatuated with Janny. She had an overwhelming woman crush, she hadn't felt like this before in her life. Looking at it now, she had been totally carried away with it.

Amy knew this would be a damaging blow to her career and to her future in the police force. She loved the job and didn't want to face the consequences of her actions. But she knew that she would have to.

What on earth was I thinking, what have I done?' Amy thought.

Amy didn't even have the excuse of being gay. It was just a major infatuation she was besotted by Janny's charisma. She'd had one hell of a woman crush, but now the reality of the situation had kicked in. Amy deeply regretted it.

It was time to face the music. She had expected DCI Chrissie Charles to summon her into her office for the inevitable confrontation. It hadn't happened yet, so she had to get in there quickly.

'*I have to try and put things right.*' Amy thought as she headed fearfully towards Chrissie's office. She reluctantly tapped on the office door. Chrissie called out for whoever was outside to enter.

'Oh it's you.' Chrissie snapped.

'Please can I have a word with you? I have to tell you why I did what I did. Amy said sheepishly.

'Come in and shut the door.'

Amy entered the office, she looked terrified. Chrissie watched her as she made her way towards her desk.

'Sit down, I haven't got much time. I have murders to investigate, in case you hadn't noticed.' Chrissie snapped. 'Go ahead but make it quick.'

'Thank you.' Amy said as she sank into the chair across from Chrissie.

Amy explained what had happened and how she had been in awe of Janny. She admitted that she had been very stupid and unprofessional in her conduct.

After Amy had explained everything, grovelling and being very apologetic. Chrissie told her that she was very lucky. She could have been immediately dismissed.

'It was all my fault, I felt so guilty, I knew that I

would have to own up and face the consequences. I couldn't let Dr Stowers take the blame for something I had done. It was all down to me. I am so very sorry. I'm definitely not gay, but I had some sort of woman crush on her. I haven't had this before in all my life and I really don't know what came over me. It was like a compulsive obsession I had. Whatever it was, I realised after trying to kiss her that it wasn't real. It was just a fantasy in my mind that I was trying to enact upon. I am so very sorry.'

'Ok, I believe you. Now get yourself back to work and I'll decide what to do with you later. In the meantime, keep your nose clean and for heaven's sake don't give me anymore grief.'

'Thank you Ma'am. I really appreciate you listening to me. I am so very sorry for what happened.'

'Ok, now go.'

Amy felt much better and relieved. She had probably ruined her career, but that didn't matter anymore. She knew she had to tell the truth. But sometimes the truth isn't always that easy to tell.

Chrissie was beginning to feel guilty herself now. What had she done? She had not only accused her wonderful partner of being unfaithful, but she had also suspected her of multiple murders.

'I am so cracking up. Nothing seems to make any sense anymore.' Chrissie thought to herself. *'I'm going to have to try and make amends with Janny. I only hope she'll forgive*

me for all the shit I've been putting her through.'

Chrissie's mind was running riot. She had been a
bloody fool. How on earth could she possibly
suspect her own partner? *'This one takes some beating.'*
Chrissie thought. She was dreading telling Janny what
had been said. She owed Janny one big fat apology.
How on earth could she put things right between
them now? She had gone in all guns blazing at Janny.
Not listening to any of her excuses and not believing
what she had told her. To top it all off, she had Janny
on the top of her suspect list. What could she
possibly do now to put things right. This was one
hell of a massive fuck up.

Chrissie sent Janny a message on messenger

'Janny, I'm so sorry. I have been a bloody stupid
fool. Can you please forgive me for my
unprofessional behaviour, and for my lack of
understanding as your partner? I can't apologise
enough for what I've said and done, and I wouldn't
blame you if you never wanted to speak to me again.
But please, I hope and pray that you will give me the
chance to put things right. I promise you that I'll try
my very best to get us back to something that
resembles our former relationship. I miss us, so
much. Chrissie.'

Chrissie sighed, she hoped it wasn't too late to
put things right between them.
There was nothing else that could be done at this
stage. She hoped Janny would reply at some point to
her message.

Chrissie went out with DI Barrow and DS Hartley to ask some questions and chase up a few leads. She had to get out for a while to take her mind off her personal life. She had important work to do, she couldn't let anything distract her from the killer. Whilst the killer was still out there, people's lives were at risk.

20

So far the information Chrissie had was minimal, not an awful lot to go on yet. There were a few leads that still needed to be followed up. CCTV coverage had been checked out and so far nothing constructive had been revealed. In the meantime she was out doing some foot work with her team. They had covered the house to house enquiries and made the relevant notes before going back to the station to write the reports.

Chrissie noticed that a message had come though from Janny. She was almost too frightened to look. She waited until she had entered her office before opening the message.

Chrissie,

I'm still very upset and disappointed in what you have accused me of. Not only do you believe that I'm capable of being unfaithful, but you also think I'm a serial killer! God help us if that's what our once stable relationship has come to. I always thought you knew me. Now I don't know what to think!

How can we possibly come back from this Chrissie? I really don't know. All I know is that I still love you, but I'm not sure that you still love me. How can you possibly love me if you believe that I am capable of having a fling with a woman as young as Amy, and in front of our colleagues.

Well to me, it means you don't trust me anymore. That's so unfair, if after all the years we've been together, that's what you could think. If you loved me, surely you would know that I am not in any way, shape or form capable of murder. I do my absolute best to save lives not take them. To think that you made me, of all people, your prime suspect in this terrible murder enquiry, in my opinion is bordering on insanity on your part. I am totally gutted! Totally! I can't just ignore this and shrug it off as though nothing has happened. I think a little space between us is necessary for now, so I can get my head around it.

I'll be in touch.
Janny x

Chrissie read the message a few times.

It was inevitable that Janny would be angry with her. Who wouldn't be? After all she deserved it, especially after what she had accused her of. So that was it then, they were having a trial separation. That night they would be apart, but not in the usual way, this time it was because their relationship was in tatters. Sleeping alone sometimes was necessary, due to work related matters. This was entirely different, they had never broken up before. It felt uncomfortable and unnatural. Would they ever be able to salvage some semblance of their former loving, sound relationship?

What the hell have I done? I am a stupid bitch, I don't deserve to have Janny as a partner. She would be better off without me. But I love her too much to let her go. I can't let her go. I'll fight tooth and nail to get her back and I'll make it up to her somehow. I've got to make her realize that I'm sorry and I don't know what I was thinking. I'll have to plead temporary insanity. Which would be true.' Chrissie thought.

She wrote a message in reply.

'My lovely Janny,

Please forgive me, I don't know what the hell I was thinking of when I sent you that awful message. It was stupid of me, of course I don't think of you as a suspect. God knows what I was thinking when I sent the message. I was jealous and angry because I thought stupidly that you were coming on to Amy. I should have known better, we have never ever been in a position where we didn't trust each other. We've always had a solid sound relationship and trusted each other, it went without saying. We were, and I truly hope we will be again, the same two women who first got together and then realized we had the perfect chemistry. We ended up being not only lovers but also best friends, a very good combination. We've continued to love and trust each other for all these years. It's all my fault, I admit I was totally out of order, I don't want to lose you Janny, I couldn't live without you. Please forgive this stupid insecure woman for ever doubting you. I know you won't believe me at the moment, but I really do love you, more than you will ever know.

I fully understand that you want some space to reflect on my totally unreasonable behaviour. I would feel the same. If you can find it in your heart to forgive me, I promise you that I will make it up to you. I'll give you some space now and when you are ready, let me know one way or the other what is to become of us. I know what I want and that is you my love.

Please, please, please forgive me.

I know I don't deserve you after what I've done but please try to find it in your heart to forgive this stupid woman. I love you so very much.

Chrissie xxx'

Chrissie sent the message and hoped that Janny would reply later.

*

Chrissie could only hope that something could be done to put things right.

Later that evening Chrissie was missing Janny, it was the time of night that they would normally unwind together. They would share a bottle of wine and make love, they'd watch DVD's or the television before retiring to bed. It was difficult to concentrate on work with her mind constantly wandering back to Janny. The whole situation had been ridiculous. Just because Janny was a heart surgeon, it didn't make her any more a suspect than any other doctor. She'd shrugged off Janny's premonitions as hocus pocus not listening to what information she had. Then when she realized that what Janny had dreamed had some truth in it. She used that as an excuse to tie her to the case, making Janny a suspect because of her inside knowledge of the murders. She had known things that only the killer would know.

'How could I have done that? Janny is my partner and I've known her for so many years. She is an excellent medical examiner and heart surgeon. I know her as a kind and caring person with a wonderful personality and she has always had the ability to make me laugh. I know for a fact she isn't capable of any of the things that I've accused her of. Why on earth did I do this to her? Will she ever forgive me? If I was her, I don't think I could forgive me.' Janny thought.

Chrissie hadn't heard from Janny since her last message stating that she wanted some space and time. She had to respect Janny's wishes, even though it took so much willpower to not send her another message. She would have to wait patiently now until Janny was ready to contact her.

Chrissie fired up her laptop and checked out a few reports and files that were connected to the murders. It helped to take her mind off Janny, even if it was only for a short period of time.

Amy Campbell was still on her list of suspects along with Janny's new assistant David Harris. Amy didn't have any medical training so she wasn't really a suspect at all. Chrissie was not using her skills, she was letting her heart rule her head. She put a line through Amy Campbell, she might be a pain in the arse but she wasn't a suspect. David Harris was in fact new to the area and had a lot of medical training, including heart surgery. He was also working closely with Janny. She didn't have any other reason to suspect him but she left him on her list. She would look into him later.

Stewart Colt was on her list, he had been released from Drayford prison well before the murders had begun. He'd been studying various medical procedures whilst he was in prison. She had arranged for a quick check into his sentence and crimes.

Apparently, Stewart Colt had been arrested and charged with drug possession and dealing. He'd been found guilty and banged up for five years. He'd had previous convictions before that, some were for drug possession along with a few other minor misdemeanours. He was also arrested for rape but the charges had been dropped because of insufficient evidence. Chrissie decided she would look into this further.

Then there was the missing psychiatric patient Mary Smithe, she hadn't been found yet. She was being very elusive and hard to locate. As far as she knew, Mary didn't have any significant medical training, but she could have been an accomplice in some way. They really do need to find her.

Chrissie checked her messages.

There was a message from David Marioni the police commissioner. Chrissie had half expected it. She read through the message, it more or less told her to get her finger out and arrest someone, preferably the killer. She replied to his message trying to fob him off for a while.

There in her inbox she noticed a new message from Janny.

Chrissie nervously opened the message, hardly daring to read its contents. She hoped it was good news and not the end of the road.

Feeling apprehensive, she perused the content.

'Chrissie,

I am missing you terribly here. It's not the same without you. I still haven't forgiven you totally, but I know deep down that you would never have accused me like that under normal circumstances. I am seriously trying to put everything into perspective. I'm attributing your unusual behaviour to the pressure and strain of working on this new complicated case. Even so, it's still a big shock to me. A huge part of me wants to get over it, I really do. A part of me wants to rush over to yours and make mad passionate love to you. But deep down I'm not ready yet to ignore the hurt and sadness that I feel inside. Give me time, and I am willing to try to salvage our former relationship. I love you very much my darling, far too much to just let us go. So please be patient for just a little while, until I am ready to resume where we left off.

I'll come into your office at some point tomorrow. We need to talk face to face. We could grab a bite to eat maybe at lunchtime.

I'll be in touch

Love you
Janny xx'

Chrissie couldn't believe it. It looks like Janny is seriously thinking about giving her another chance.

She would wait as long as it takes. At least she would have the chance to try and explain. But how could she explain when she didn't know herself why she had behaved in that stupid, idiotic, ridiculous and unforgivable way towards Janny.

Chrissie sent her a reply, she really hoped that they could regain their wonderful relationship. My God, this should never have happened, and it was all her own fault. She couldn't apologize enough. Chrissie hoped that Janny would accept her apology, as it was intended, straight from the heart.

For the rest of the evening, Chrissie concentrated on her work. She checked out some more details from the information already gathered regarding Stewart Colt. He had apparently used his time in prison to research various medical procedures. He had informed prison staff that he wanted to go straight after being released. He'd been allowed some limited access to the Internet and used it to look up medical information. He also spent a lot of his free time in the library studying. He went into medical training as soon as he was released from prison. It appeared that Stewart Colt was serious about going straight. He managed to get a job in a private heart hospital. Chrissie decided, he was certainly a candidate for her updated suspect list.

Chrissie looked through some information they had about David Harris. He was new to the area and apparently he had a twin sister. David was a very highly trained and skilled doctor who was specializing in forensic science. He was a great asset to Janny's department. Chrissie would like to know who his twin sister was.

Quickly she scribbled a note to remind her to

check the identity of his twin sister. For the rest of
the evening she waded through the many reports.

21

The following morning.

Janny went to work as usual in the hospital. David Harris had informed her that Dr. Katherine Garfield had been covering her cases in her absence. He put some files on her desk with the updated medical coverage done by Dr. Garfield.

'Thank you David, much appreciated. You have been a great help to me.'

'No problem Dr. Stowers. I'm glad to be able to help you, it's a privilege for me to be to be a part of your work. I have always admired what you do.'

'Thank you.'

'No Dr. Stowers, thank you.'

Janny read through the notes that Dr. Garfield had left for her. She had every faith in Katherine, she was a very good heart surgeon, and in fact she would rate her as one of the best there is. Janny felt it was a privilege that she would come in and cover for her. She picked up the phone and called her. She wanted to thank her personally for what she had done. Janny thanked Dr. Garfield for stepping in for her.

'Any time Dr. Stowers, if I am free, I really don't mind. I would love for us to get together sometime and discuss our respective work related issues. It would be a pleasure.'

'That would be lovely Dr. Garfield, we'll have to arrange that in the not too distant future.' Janny replied.

Janny picked up her mobile and sent Chrissie a text message. She had missed her so much last night, it seemed so unnatural. It wouldn't be easy for either of them to try to carry on as normal again. She knew it wouldn't be easy on her part to forgive and forget what Chrissie had said and accused her of. Janny knew that in order for their relationship to flourish again, they would both have to try to resolve the issues between them. Life wouldn't be the same without each other. It went without saying that they both loved each other dearly. It would be a crying shame if they just gave up on their relationship.

Chrissie was in her office. She had just finished the team briefing. They had been briefed, dismissed and sent on their way to their allotted investigative assignments. She was sipping at a cup of coffee that Sally had brought in for her earlier, it was almost cold now. Her mind had started to wander again, to thoughts of Janny. Chrissie had fully intended to concentrate on her work, there were files on her desk that needed her attention. She'd become distracted by her thoughts, as if they were on a loop tape, they had been constantly bombarding and preying on her mind. She realised just how unfair and awful she had been towards Janny. There was no excuse for what she had put Janny through.

'Would I have forgiven Janny if it had been the other way round? I really don't know. It would be very difficult to forget the hurtful accusations. I would have found it very hard. How could I have put her through that?' Chrissie thought to herself.

She heard the sound of an incoming text message. It was from Janny.

'Hi Chrissie,

Is it ok to come to your office in about half an hour? I know you are extremely busy but we really need to talk. If you can manage about an hour that would be great. We could go for an early lunch.

I love you, my screwed up DCI.
xxxx.'

Chrissie smiled at the end remark. How she yearned for them to get back to normal, she missed Janny so much.

She sent a text in return agreeing to meet up. She hoped that she could convince Janny that it had been a stupid lapse of sense on her part. It was unforgivable and extremely hurtful towards Janny. Chrissie wished she could turn the clock back. All she can do now is grovel and apologise in the hope Janny can bring herself to forgive her.

*

The two women sat across from each other in Jack's café. They had ordered a coffee and a sandwich each. There was so much to discuss in such a short space of time. It was very important that they get everything out into the open before things started to fester.

'I am so very sorry Janny. You have no idea how sorry I am. I know it doesn't do anything to take back the stupid words and the totally unfounded accusations I made. I don't even know why I felt like that. I haven't got any reasons or excuses for my behaviour. None what so ever. I wouldn't blame you if you never forgave me, but I hope against all hope that you can forgive and forget all that shit. I fucked up big time.' Chrissie told her.

'I think a lot of it was stress related Chrissie. I've known you long enough to know that wasn't the Chrissie I know and love. Having said that, it really did hurt me.'

'I know, I wish I could wave a magic wand and take it all away but I can't, the damage has been done and I don't know what to do to put it right.'

'OK, I have been thinking about it seriously and I have come to the conclusion that we are above all this shit. This I think, has been exacerbated by the sudden jealousy you've recently been experiencing. The rest has just escalated from that. There is no room in our relationship for any negative emotions, jealousy being one of them. We have enough negativity in our professions without having extra stress in our relationship. It's one of the reason's we have stayed together as a couple for so long. We have always had the love, sex, and trust to keep us sane in what would otherwise be an insane life. I don't think either of us could survive without the love and support we give each other.'

'Janny, how can I put this right? What can I do to show you that I truly love you above everything else? I'll do anything I possibly can to get us back on track. I'm so sorry about everything. I've let you down so badly. I shouldn't have even contemplated accusing you of anything. I know you are not capable of any of the totally unfounded accusations I threw at you.'

'Chrissie, what's done is done, we're going to have to try and laugh it off and move on from this. Yes, we must laugh it off, it's what we do. Otherwise it will keep cropping up in arguments. We have to move on as soon as possible, and put it all down to experience. If you ever feel the slightest bit jealous again, you need to talk to me and we'll try and sort it out straight away Jealousy isn't something either of us usually suffers from. I think the stress following the stamp master case, and now these latest murders, have all contributed in some way. All these factors are detrimental to our state of mind. Having said that, we're still the same people we were before. We are both probably a little bit scared from it. We must never let anything like this get in the way of our relationship ever again. Hey I'm no shrink, but I think if we follow our hearts we won't go far wrong. What do you think?' Janny asked.

'I think you are fucking marvellous Janny

Stowers. I don't deserve you, but I love you and respect you so much.'

'Right, we deserve each other Chrissie, we trust each other. We love each other and have mad, passionate sex with each other. We work on cases together and work well as a team in our working relationship as well as our personal one. We have so much going for us, as long as we have each other darling. Don't ever forget that.' Janny told her as they made their way back towards the police station.

The desk sergeant John Baker waved Chrissie across to the desk.

'There's been another body found. It was called in a few moments ago. DI Barrow, DS Hartley and DS Trivett are on their way there now ma'am.'

'Oh shit, not another one, can you get me a car and driver right away.'

The sergeant made a call to arrange for the vehicle. Janny knew the forensic team would have already been called out and informed of the incident.

The two women both arrived at the scene in the car that had been provided. The first response team had already sealed off the area. The body of a woman had been dumped on the side of the road. There wasn't any signs of this being connected in any way to the previous murders. It could mean that they had two killers on the loose. How unlucky was that.

'OK, what have we got here?' Chrissie asked DI

James Barrow.

'The victim is female, has a stab wound to the chest. Her face has been badly beaten. Looks like she has been raped or sexually assaulted going by the condition of her clothes. I would guess at her being in her late twenties or thereabouts. First response have cordoned off the area and forensics are on the case as we speak.' James informed Chrissie.

DS Hartley and DS Trivett were both making notes in their notebooks.

'Thanks, we're going to check out the body now.' She replied.

Janny and Chrissie had both donned coverall's, gloves and overshoes. Then they made their way towards the cordoned off area to inspect the corpse.

'Tell me this is not happening.' Chrissie said to Janny as they walked towards the scene.

'I'm afraid it is.' Janny told her.

Janny worked alongside the forensic team to gather any information or clues as to what happened to the victim. Once the forensic and photographic evidence gathering was complete. The body was bagged along with all the trace evidence at the scene. The team had to document everything along with the timescales. She would be going to the morgue later to examine the body further and perform the post-mortem.

'I'm going back to the morgue with the body now. I'll try to find out as much as I can and I'll let you have the information a.s.a.p. I'll call you later and we can meet up, have something to eat and then maybe we could share a bottle of wine together at yours if that's ok with you.'

'I would love that Janny. Thank you for being so understanding. I love you very much, you know that don't you?'

'Of course I know. I love you too, I always will, you know that don't you?'

'Yes my darling, I know, I wouldn't be me without you. You complete me.' Chrissie replied as she got into the squad car. 'Now I really must get back to the station to try to solve all these bloody murders. I appear to be collecting them.'

22

Chrissie set up an extra white board for the new victim. It wasn't the same killer, this murder didn't have anything at all to tie them together. She knew that she would have to treat it as a separate case.

Sally rang Chrissie's extension number.

'I've got DS Hartley on the line for you.'

'Thanks Sally, put him through.'

'We've got an ID on the stabbing victim. She was Jane Stevens, aged 25. She worked as a prostitute, and had been reported missing by her fellow streetwalkers. She apparently worked in the Lockington red light area.'

'Great work, now I'll need to gather all the information we can get about her. Can you and your team interview the people who knew her for me please?'

'No problem, I'll get back to you on that. DS Trivett is working on this with me, along with PC Campbell, is that ok with you?'

'Yes, that's fine, if I need any of you for something else I'll just pull you out. Tell PC

Campbell, she can work the case with you until
further notice.' Chrissie told him, she had decided to
give Amy Campbell another chance. She'd better be
bloody well grateful and not balls it up.

Chrissie asked Sally to contact Cheryl Teal, she
would need a profile of this latest killer. A meeting
was arranged.

Janny had been busy working with the forensic
team.

The rest of the day was spent gathering
information and interviewing people who knew the
dead woman. Janny was working closely with her
forensic team. She visited the technicians in the lab
to try and get any early results. Sue Kelly was looking
through a microscope as Janny entered. Sue said hi
with a quick glance as she entered. Darren Bailey was
one of the technicians there who specialised in toxins,
he had some feedback from the initial toxicology
tests.

'We've got some traces of Suxamethonium
chloride as you know induces muscle relaxation. We
also found some traces of Sodium Pentathol known
as the truth drug, sometimes used as an anaesthetic.
These were present in all the three heartless murder
victims. I've completed my initial report and faxed it
through to DCI Charles.'

'Thanks Darren, that's great, I'm sure it will help
us to piece together some clues as to what happened
to the victims before, during and after the abductions.
So Alan Denning, David Blackstock and Neil Jordan

all had the same traces of drugs when tested. That's interesting, the killer obviously had access to these drugs.'

'True, but they could have been bought on the Internet by the killer. It's relatively easy these days, in fact there isn't much you can't get on the net nowadays. Frightening though it is.' Darren told her.

'Can I have a copy of the tox reports, I'll do some research online. I'll check how to easy it is to obtain these drugs. You never know, I might just hit on to something. Do we have the computer hard drives of any of the victims Darren?'

'I think the IT department have already received the laptops and are working on them. Megan Short will let you know if anything of importance turns up. They will have to crack the passwords first, then they will check into the history, which more than likely will have been deleted. But it can usually be retrieved by the experts. David Johnson and Gabby Finch are both in today if you want to get in touch with them.' Darren informed Janny.

Janny thanked the team and put the reports in her briefcase before leaving.

Making her way to the IT department, Janny stopped for a few moments to send Chrissie a text.

23

DCI Charles had just finished speaking to Cheryl Teal on the phone. Cheryl had promised Chrissie that she would provide a profile based on the information she had been given. They had arranged to meet up once the report was complete so they could discuss the killer's possible motive for raping and murdering Jane Stevens.

Chrissie heard the fax machine spring into life. Sally came into the office with a multi-page fax. The tox reports had arrived. She wasn't surprised that all three victims had been drugged. It was how the victims had been subdued and controlled when they had been taken.

Sally put a call through to Chrissie. It was David Marioni the police commissioner. He wanted to know the details of the latest killing. He wasn't very happy that no one had been arrested for the Heartless killings. Chrissie cursed him under her breath.

Chrissie gathered all the information she had so far on the rape victim. Added any relevant pointers onto the new white board that had been set up for Jane Stevens. That done, she checked the other white board which displayed the heartless murders information.

Just then her phone signalled an incoming text. It was from Janny.

'Thank goodness, I still have Janny. No matter what happens, I'll cope. As long as I have Janny to support me I know I'll be ok. I'm so lucky, so very, very, lucky.' She thought to herself.

Chrissie read the message and then sent one back.

'Hi Chrissie,

I know you're busy but I thought you might like to know that I'm here for you if you need me for anything. I'll see you later darling. I love you very much. Can't wait for later when we can chill together with a nice relaxing tipple of wine and maybe a little sexual healing wouldn't go amiss eh?

Yours forever
Janny xxxx'

A tear fell from Chrissie's eye as she read the lovely words Janny had said in the message. She was happy, even though the murders hadn't been solved. She knew that with Janny' help they would get through this. It felt real, it felt right.

'Hi Janny,

Thank you for sending me that lovely message. It has probably saved me from going insane lol. Your words touched me, thank you so much Janny for being there. I can't wait to unwind with you later. I love you very much darling.

Love Chrissie xxxx.'

Janny had gathered some information from the IT department on the heartless killings. Alan Denning had a Twitter, a Facebook and Instagram account. Not surprising really with him being a young med student.

David Blackstock, the teacher had Facebook and LinkedIn accounts. Neil Jordan the electrician had an old Facebook account which he hadn't used or updated since he had separated from his wife. Nothing significant was uncovered from checking out the sites and pages the victims had used. It could be that the victims didn't know the killer.

Megan Short, the consultant IT manager had told her that they were still checking for more sites the victims might have visited. David Johnson and Gabby French were also working on the laptop hard drives. Janny thanked them and left with the reports.

Janny read the message Chrissie had sent to her. She smiled to herself, life is definitely improving by the minute.

24

Tanya Colleen had noticed the man watching her as she danced in the club where she worked as a lap dancer. It had only meant to be a temporary job to get her through, to provide some money until she could find something better. She wasn't getting any younger and now in her mid-thirties, it was time to slow down and move on. Time wasn't on her side anymore. Her body had provided the skills for her lap dancing job. She was still a looker, but she was aware that she wouldn't stay like this forever. Tanya had been attending college and was applying for what she described as proper jobs now. Her lack of experience was holding her back. There wasn't much call for office workers with lap dancing experience. She wasn't going to give up, she would join an agency if nothing came up soon. At least she would gain some experience in the workplace that way, and who knows, it may lead to a permanent position.

The man, in his mid-thirties, was waiting in his car, he called out to Tonya as she left the club via the back door.

'Hey darling, would you like a lift?' He asked.

'No thanks, I'll walk back, it keeps me fit.'

'You're fit enough darling. How about a quick coffee? I know a very nice place, we could go there and it would give you the chance to unwind a bit before going home. What do you say?' He asked her. 'No strings, and I'll either drive you home or you can walk, it's entirely up to you.'

Tanya went against all her previous safety rules by accepting the invitation of a coffee. After all, there was no harm in that was there? She was feeling her age and an invitation from a not too bad looking man had boosted her ego and her mood.

'OK then, just a quick coffee, then I really must go.' She told him.

'Get in, it's just down the road from here. It looks a bit like rain, no point in getting wet.'

She opened the passenger door and got into his car and he drove off. He turned off the main road and into a dirt road, that's when Tanya realized they were not going to go for a coffee.

'Where are you taking me?' Tanya asked him nervously.

She was beginning to get alarmed now. He stopped the car.

'Shut up bitch.' He said as he punched her in the mouth. Blood spurted from her lips where the punch had sent her teeth forcibly through them. The pain was immense, a few teeth had been loosened and fell out with the blood as she spat out the excess

'Why are you doing this?'

'Because I can.' He told her.

'Please stop, don't hurt me anymore. I'll do anything you say but please stop……please.' She pleaded.

'Shut your fucking ugly bloody mouth you slutty bitch. You will get what's coming to you. Say goodbye sweet world, because yours is coming to a befitting end

He hit her over and over again until her face was a bloody mess. Tanya's panties were dragged down to her knees as he pushed his fingers inside her.

'Scream for me bitch.'

He forced his erect penis deep and hard inside her. He continued to beat and rape her until he had satisfied his violent and sexual needs.

Tanya knew that she wasn't going to survive this. She was right. As the knife entered her heart her life ebbed away and came to an abrupt halt.

25

That evening Chrissie and Janny relaxed together. They had eaten in town and then gone back to Chrissie's. It seemed a bit strange at first, but then it was so nice to unwind together just like they always did following a long hard day. The best part of falling out was the making up. They had made love and it was the best sex they had experienced in years. Not that they had bad sex, far from it. Sex between the two women had never been an issue or a problem. Tonight it was like they had met for the very first time. They were both relaxed with each other once more. It was going to be ok.

'I know you don't like me mentioning it Chrissie but I've had another dream. I really want to tell you about them. Just in case they might help to lead us in the right or general direction. They might not help at all, but every little detail that's missed is another chance for the killer to kill again.'

'You're right Janny, I will listen to what you have to say and take on board anything that could help. I can't use it in a documented way but at least I can hear what you have to say.'

'That's all I ask Chrissie. I would never forgive myself if I had information following a dream or premonition, if I hadn't told you and it could have been important.'

'Ok, Janny, I promise that I'll listen to everything you have to say. It can't do any harm and it might prove to be very useful or even vital to the cases we are working on. I'm sorry if I made you feel bad about your dreams. It was just so difficult to get my head around. If I'm honest it still feels very weird.'

'I can understand that, but all I ask is for you to keep an open mind about it.'

'I promise I will. It's the least I can do after putting you through hell.'

Janny spent a little while explaining what she had seen in her last dream which was apparently a dark haired woman in her early thirties. The killer had dark hair and appeared to be in his thirties she told Chrissie. They were in a car when the woman was raped then stabbed in the heart. The killer dumped her body by the roadside then drove off. Janny had described the first woman victim, who had been raped and murdered by this new killer, previously and it had been very accurate. This latest dream was about a woman they had not yet discovered. Time would undoubtedly uncover the truth.

It was so uncanny Chrissie thought, but there appeared to be a lot of truth and fact about what she was telling her. Very strange.

'Anyway, thanks for the info much appreciated darling but can we get back to the important stuff.'

'Hmmm, I think you must mean you would like your glass topping up. Maybe I could top you up a bit too eh?'

'Janny, you can top me up anytime you like, along with my wine. I love you so much.'

Janny topped up Chrissie's wine glass along with her own. She edged towards her and parted her dressing gown to allow her to gain access. Then she began to top Chrissie up too.

Chrissie moaned as she felt the orgasm rising, the heat waves then the pulsating waves, invaded her body. She was on a sea of sexual arousal, in which she was drowning. There was no going back, the orgasm had reached the point of no return, it was taking over her whole body as she climaxed, she screamed out loud with total ecstasy. Oh how she had missed this. It had only been one night of separation. That had been more than enough to make them both realise how much they needed each other.

They finished off the wine and following their mad passionate, sexual healing techniques, they made their way to bed. They were both totally relaxed now. It would be short lived though because the latest murder was yet another mystery that needed to be solved. Chrissie snored as she drifted off to sleep.

It was important DCI Chrissie Charles thought, to get all the information she could accumulate, in order to catch these heartless murdering bastards.

26

Stewart and the Bear

Stewart Colt was getting flashbacks of his time in prison. He got them periodically. Not very nice memories of his life in the hellhole called Drayfield prison.

The first night he had spent in prison was fairly uneventful. Stewart settled in and had a good night's sleep. He could cope with this he thought. As long as he kept his nose clean, he could do his time and maybe utilise the time he was in prison constructively. He'd decided to spend his free time inside wisely, he could study medical subjects. He'd always been drawn in that direction but he had never had the chance. This could possibly be his vocation, it could well be a blessing in disguise, him being banged up.

The following morning Stewart made his way to the showers. He hung his towel on the hook provided. The torrents of water felt warm and relaxing as it cascaded down his soapy body.

Stewart stepped out of the shower and was drying himself when three large men entered. One of the men was extremely huge. He stood in the middle of the other two large men. They looked very intimidating, Stewart felt uneasy.

Stewart had wrapped the towel around his waist and moved to leave the showers. He tried to go around the men, but the three large men had blocked his exit.

The man in the middle was a huge black African male who apparently had been nick named 'The Bear.'

The bear pointed towards the shower cubicle and smiled at him. His two escorts grabbed Stewart's arms one at either side of him and roughly forced him back into the cubicle. He tried to struggle but it was totally useless against these men. A profound fear of what was about to happen overcame him. He was outnumbered with no way of escaping.

The bear dropped his towel exposing a penis befitting his nickname. Stewart was aware that something awful was about to happen.

'Don't struggle, it will hurt much more if you do.' The bear told him as he soaped his penis. 'The soap will make it slide in better.'

'Hold him tight boys, bend him over. You my lovely, you must brace yourself, and try to relax.' The bear said.

'Fuck you.' Stewart told him.

'No, I get to fuck you.' The bear told him as he yanked at Stewart's towel and threw it on the floor, then stroked his backside in a sensual and sexual manner. He took hold of Stewart's penis and stroked it gently. You are going to grow to love me darling.'

'Relax. This is my little treat to you. You are very highly honoured. I am very particular who I fuck.'

'Piss off bastard.'

The two men holding him forced him forward until he was pinned right up against the cubicle wall. They turned on the shower.

The bear forced himself inside a screaming Stewart. The water running down the shower's drain turned to a diluted red.

The bear slapped Stewart on his bum as he was leaving. Stewart was hurting; he wasn't looking forward to the many frequent rapes he would have to endure in this hellhole.

'I'll see you again soon. I like you. You're now my bitch. You take care of my needs and I'll make sure you're safe in here.'

The bear had kept his word, Stewart had never been intimidated or hassled by any other inmate. He belonged to the bear, no one would cross him.

27

Mike Hartley and Sharon Trivott were eating their evening meal before retiring to Mike's place for the rest of the evening. It had been a long day, they were unwinding with good food and fine wine.

'I can't believe we have another killer on the loose as well as the heartless murderer. How unlucky is that, I feel so sorry for DCI Charles. It can't be easy organising homicide investigations. One is bad enough but it now looks like we have two.' Sharon said to Mike as he finished off his wine.

'I wouldn't like to be in charge at this moment in time, that's for sure. I'm glad that DCI Charles is in charge, she knows what she's doing. All we can do is make sure we follow her instructions and help her wherever we can. Anyway that's enough about work. I want to get you home so I can have my wicked way with you. Once that door has closed when we get back I'm going to have you right there darling. Now what do you think about that?'

'In your dreams Mikey boy, you can wait until I'm good and ready.'

'We'll see.'

'Yep, we'll see.'

*

The surgeon was not happy. So much still to do and time was getting short. Soon the surgeon knew that this would all have to end. No more operations after this last attempt. Just one more go at it, then its game over.

The nurse Gabby Fielding was desperate to try to find a way out of this. She was planning her escape, it was all she could think about because there was nothing else to do in her makeshift cell. She'd spent many hours thinking about escaping. It was not going to be easy; her chain shackles were attached to the old curtain partition rail, which was once part of a four-bed ward. The chain was long enough for her to reach the toilet and sink area, which was something she supposed. The only time she was released from the chains was when she had to assist in the operations. Then she was allowed to get into her scrubs. She was never left alone and was threatened of what would happen if she tried to escape. If she had the opportunity, she knew that there would only be one shot at it. No room for any errors.

Mary Smithe was frightened, but the voices had told her to stay calm. She was going to investigate later, she would have to be very careful not to make a noise or let anyone know she was there. The voices agreed.

*

'Get your kit off Hartley.' Sharon Trivott ordered.

'Anything to oblige you my darling.' Mike replied as he struggled out of his trousers.

He was hopping about on one leg trying to speed up the process without much success.

Sharon laughed at him as she removed her clothes and jumped onto the bed. She was teasing Mike by spreading her legs wide open.

'Come and get me.'

Mike gave up on the trousers and jumped onto the bed with one leg still in them and the other leg loose. Finally he managed to wriggle out of them.

'Oopps you missed the moment.' Sharon said as she shut her legs.

'Oh bugger, you cruel woman, how can you do this to me.'

'It's easy, Mikey boy. If you play your cards right I might just let you in……' Mike was already in. 'Ohh you crafty sod, how did you do that?'

'I've had years of practice and now I get to try out everything I know on you.'

'Not only are you cradle snatching, you are using and abusing me.' Sharon said as Mike turned her over and re-entered her from the rear.

'You don't seem to be struggling, would you like me to stop?'

'Oh for fuck's sake, noooo don't stop, just get on with it. Ohhhh yes, that's it, yes that's it…'

They made love like it was their very last time. The couple had successfully wound down from the stresses of the working day. They could, for the moment, forget about the murder investigations. They slept fitfully, contentedly and blissfully in each other's arms. Tomorrow was still a long way off.

28

Chrissie was determined to make some headway today. She had the tox reports and the post-mortem results in front of her. Janny had provided some information from her dream of the roadside murder victim. It was obvious that the heartless murderer didn't kill the latest murder victim.

Cheryl Teal had just arrived. Sally ushered her into the interview room. She returned with tea, coffee and biscuits.

'Thanks for coming at such short notice Cheryl, anything at all you can give me is much appreciated. I am drowning in a sea of murder victims at the moment.'

'I'm inclined to agree with you, that it's highly unlikely the roadside victim has anything to do with the heartless killer. The killer in this case is committing the crime with a lot of built up passion and anger. It could be that a woman has let him down or abused him in some way. The killer could have come from a broken home. As things stand at the moment, it's a random rape and murder case, which appears to have no apparent reason or motive. That in its self means there has been some sort of trigger. Either that or the killer has suffered some sort of degrading sexual encounter. It could be that it's something that the killer had begun years ago. So it might be worth putting a few feelers out about rape victims over the last ten years or so. It's a long shot I know, but something might just pop out at you while you're checking.'

'I'll get someone on to it straight away, thanks Cheryl.'

'No problem, I've done a quick report for you in more detail, based solely on the facts we already know so far.'

Cheryl handed Chrissie the report before leaving. Chrissie checked her suspect list and one name popped up. She would check out Stewart Colt and find out just what he'd been up to since his release from prison.

'Mike, can you check out Stewart Colt for me? He served time in Drayford prison. He did a five year stretch for drug related offenses. Check to see if he had any regular visitors etc.'

'Will do ma'am. I've already made a start on it because I thought he would be one of the main suspects in the case.'

'Great stuff, let me know as soon as you have anything constructive.'

Chrissie checked out Amy Campbell's personal file and looked into David Harris's personal file.

'Hmmm, that's interesting. Both Amy and David

had a twin, I wonder…..' Chrissie thought.

She waited until the end of Amy's shift and summoned her into her office.

Amy walked in sheepishly. She didn't know what to expect from DCI Charles anymore. She was lucky to have a job at all after what she had done. Thankfully Chrissie had been very understanding so she wanted to make a better impression now. She was worried that she may have done something wrong and that was why she had been called in to Chrissie's office.

'Take a seat PC Campbell.' Chrissie said as she shuffled the papers on her desk. 'I'd like to ask you a few questions. It says on your personal file that you have a twin brother but it doesn't mention your twin brother's name.'

'Yes ma'am, I do have a twin brother. His name is David Harris and he works with Dr. Stowers.'

'Can you tell me why you don't share the same surname?'

'It was David who changed his name. He didn't like to be associated with our dad Jeremy Campbell. David had been scrounging money off dad for expenses while he was at university studying medicine. Dad had always paid his tuition fees, but he had refused to fund his increasingly expensive social life. Dad got fed up of being screwed, so he told him to get a job to fund his playboy lifestyle. They'd never really got on, after that. We are ok as a family now and we all meet up at Christmas etc. But David never really relaxes when he visits the family.'

'I see, do you see much of David?' Chrissie asked.

'Not really, we used to be very close but since we went on our different career paths we grew apart. I've seen him a lot more since we moved closer with our work.' He lives in Drayfield and I live in Lockington.'

'Thank you for that Amy, now go home and try to unwind before your shift tomorrow afternoon.'

Amy was relieved once she knew that it wasn't anything to do with her work. She breathed a sigh of relief as she left the station.'

29

Janny was tired, she just wanted to go home and chill with Chrissie. That was always a great way of unwinding. There was nothing better than a nice meal followed by wine and sex, not necessarily in that order.

She had sent a text to Chrissie. They'd made arrangements to meet up later, and planned to go out and have a nice meal before going back to her place. Janny had popped into the supermarket earlier, to get them some wine for the evening. Everything was in place for when they returned. It promised to be a nice relaxing contrast to their day.

Janny felt much better about their relationship now. Chrissie had gone out of her way to apologise. This was more than enough to remind her just how much they both needed each other. No matter what happened between them, or however many arguments and disagreements they had, they would always remain very close. They were meant for each other, they were soul mates and nothing could change that. They were both aware of the bond they were lucky enough to share.

Janny was finishing off her paperwork before leaving the hospital. There was a knock on her office door.

'Come in.'

Carol, Janny's secretary walked into the office carrying a box.

'This came for you earlier, I haven't seen you since to give it to you.'

'No probs Carol, just pop it on the desk, I'll check it out before I leave.'

Janny stared at the box, she had a bad feeling, she didn't know why, but she knew that for some reason she wouldn't like the contents.

After the paperwork was completed, Janny turned her attention to the package which was perched on the edge of her desk. She still didn't feel good about opening it.

'For God's sake Janny get a bloody grip! It's probably a box full of medical samples left by one of the reps.' She thought.

She carefully slit the tape on the box and opened it cautiously. Inside the package was an insulated cooler box, which contained a selection of human hearts. There were four hearts in total. These were not samples, these were meant to shock her. Why?

Janny rang Chrissie straight away and asked her to arrange a crime scene investigation team. She explained what had happened and Chrissie told her they were on their way. Janny had arranged for a team of forensics to attend. This could be vital evidence, it was important not to allow it to get contaminated. She suited up and set to work on searching for any vital clues that might point to where the hearts had come from. She instinctively knew that once the DNA tests had been performed, it would prove that these hearts were a present from the 'Heartless Killer.' Things were definitely on a downhill spiral, going from bad to worse.

*

'This is so gross, why on earth would the killer want to send you these hearts?' Chrissie said as she stepped out of her suit and placed it in a bag so forensics could check for any trace evidence.

'These I think are the surgeon's trophies, a little keep sake. As you know this can be quite common in serial killings. I just don't know why the killer would want to send them to me!'

'Well let's get these all bagged up and sent to the lab. With a bit of luck, we might have some more evidence to go on after this. Well, I hope so anyway.

'Most people get chocolates, or flowers in their deliveries, me I get a bloody box full of dead hearts. What a bummer eh.'

'Never mind Janny, I'll get you flowers and chocolates and I'll throw in a bottle of wine. Once we've caught the killer we'll celebrate in style.'

'Sounds good to me Chrissie, I'll take you up on that.'

30

Following the various forensic tests, the hearts had eventually been identified as a match to the three heartless murder victims, all except for one

'The fourth heart doesn't have a matching body. That means we have three of the bodies but not a fourth. It also means there has been another heartless murder and we haven't discovered the body yet.' Chrissie told Janny over their evening meal in the Travellers Rest.

It was their favourite eating place in Sheffield's City Centre.

'I dread to think who this surgeon is. Whoever it is, this person is very dangerous and clever with it. Shit, what a combination. I'm not happy about the fact that the surgeon sent the hearts to you. After last time, the last thing I want is for you to be at risk again. Whatever happens don't interfere in this case on your own. You must have back up at all times. I don't want you to do any of your investigative interfering on your own. If you have any information of any kind, whether you think it's important or not. You must let me or the team know and we'll look into anything important together. So please Janny, please don't take any unnecessary risks. Keep me informed at all times.'

'Chrissie, I promise I won't take any unnecessary chances. I've learnt from my mistakes.'

The two women finished their meal and drank their wine. They headed off to Chrissie's place where they spent the rest of the night relaxing together, making love and generally chilling. Tomorrow they would make an early start. There was still a lot of investigating to do.

'Would you like a top up?' Chrissie asked.

'Oh you cheeky devil, what sort of top up are we talking about this time eh? We seem to be having regular top ups lately.'

'Well for starters we could top up our wine glasses, what do you think?'

'Ok, it sounds like a plan. We mustn't have too much though, we're in for another hectic and long day tomorrow.'

'We'll worry about tomorrow when it comes. You know what they say, tomorrow never comes.'

'We wish Chrissie, we wish.'

'Are you ready for another top up?' Chrissie asked as she put her hand inside Janny's dressing gown.

'Just the one.' Janny said as they made love again.

It was nice to get their lives back on track. They were returning to the people they had been, before the awful rot had set in. Now they were together again in every sense of the word, they wouldn't be allowing anything or anyone to part them. They were strong together and they were united as a couple, as a team they could conquer anything.

31

The rape murder and the heartless murders were causing a lot of media attention. To top it all off, now they had a box of miscellaneous hearts. David Marioni was being hassled by the press. He would have to get DCI Chrissie Charles to up her game. This wouldn't do at all.

'The commissioner has been ringing all morning, trying to get hold of you. I've put him off a few times making excuses, but I think he's getting rather annoyed now. You might have to speak to him. If you don't, he'll probably pay us a visit, and I don't think that would be very productive at the moment.' Sally told Chrissie.

'Ok, thanks Sally, I'll give him a call and get the ear bashing over with. Then I've got to go out with the team. Can you let DS Hartley and DI Barrow on the phone and ask them to pick me up before leaving. I'll sort out Commissioner Marioni now.

'DCI Charles, I'm very disappointed in the way you are handling this case. Nothing constructive has been done as yet. I've got the media on my back and I've got nothing to give them. Give me some answers, I need answers and arrests. Pull out all the stops and get me a killer in custody or there will be consequences.'

He hung up leaving Chrissie reeling from his booming voice.

'Well mister, when I've got the answers, you might get some.' She thought. *'Until then you can sod right off.'*

'The shit is beginning to hit the fan.' Chrissie thought.

She was fuming inside.

'How dare he try his bloody bullying tactics on me? It won't change anything, it will only make me angrier. He's an idiot.'

Chrissie set off with her team; there were interviews to conduct and door-to-door enquiries to execute.

'Hi ho, hi ho, it's off to work I go.' She sang to herself.

She had managed to send a quick text to Janny before setting out. Chrissie smiled when she got the rude reply. Thank God for Janny.

32

The surgeon was not very confident at all, things were going from bad to worse. It would only be a matter of time before the police would realize that the murders had a purpose. Then with a little research it would soon be discovered the true identity of the surgeon and of the people who were involved.

Dr Janny Stowers was definitely a force to be reckoned with. She was no idiot. It had been intentional on the surgeon's assistant's part to send the hearts to her. It might just buy that little bit of time they needed to finish off and get the hell out before being discovered. It would be touch and go. Things were becoming desperate.

The last heart transplant was the only hope for the young man who desperately needed the heart. It was all coming to an end. The young man was dying and there were no other options open. It was only a matter of time before his diseased heart would stop beating.

This was now the end. A quick clean up and a quick escape was all that was left.

*

Mary was still in two minds as to what she should do for the best. Having now seen the operating theatre, she knew that the surgeon was not legitimate, the operations were done under extremely unorthodox conditions.

She had to decide quickly what she should do. There were a few options but all of them contained an element of risk. She could inform the police, this option would be the best she thought, but then she would have to leave her new home. Thinking about it there were no other real options, because whatever happened she would have to leave anyway. It was dangerous here, that she knew, and the voices had already warned her to get the hell out of there.

She went out and made her way to the pub where she ordered something to eat. Mary sat in a dark corner eating, drinking and thinking. The voices told her to inform the police, it was the right thing to do. She would do that later.

First she had to return to pick up her few possessions, they were all she had in the world along with her voices of course. She had become obsessively possessive of her belongings. The voices warned her that she was playing a very dangerous game. Mary was afraid, she feared for her life, but she had to go back.

*

Another body is discovered

Chrissie was called out when another body was discovered on the roadside between Hairdale and Lockington. Janny had instantly recognised the victim from her dream. The woman had dark hair as in her dream and had been very badly beaten. Then finally, she had been stabbed in the heart.

It was exactly how Janny had described it from

her dream. There was no denying it, Janny's dreams were some sort of premonitions.

'What the fuck is going on here?' Chrissie asked the team.

'We've got another rape and murder case on our hands by the looks of it.' DS Hartley told her.

'Why on earth do I get all the shitty cases? Its bad enough trying to solve one murder, let alone all these fucking bodies that appear to be coming out of the woodwork. There are two different types of murders going on here. Looks like I've got two separate serial killers. Shit, what are the odds of that happening? What the hell am I supposed to do now.'

'We're working on it ma'am, whoever is involved with these murders, were going to nail them. They won't get away with it. We're pulling out all the stops, no stone will be left unturned. We are on this.' DI Barrow told her.

The forensic team had collected as much source information as possible from the cordoned off site. All the usual procedures had been followed to collect any evidence which may be vital later to be used in court. Janny made her way to the morgue with the body once it had been released. By assessing the body at the scene Janny was convinced that this murder had been committed by the same killer as the last roadside murder. So it could be there are two serial killers on the loose here. Poor Chrissie certainly would have her work cut out with all these murder victims.

'Can you guys check out any CCTV footage? I'll get on to the lab and insist on a quick outcome from the tests.'

'We're on it ma'am.'

'Oh, and can we get the missing persons list checked for this victim please. I really can't believe this fucking shit.' Chrissie told them.

'Consider it done ma'am.' DI James Barrow assured her.

'Try not to get too stressed Chrissie, just remember how good you are and just concentrate on your job. Everyone is behind you on this, including me.' Janny told her.

'I know, I've got a fantastic team of detectives and a wonderful partner and ME on-board. It's a piece of cake, isn't it? Goes without saying really, it won't be long before we get these bastards. God help them when we do.' Chrissie replied.

33

Chrissie was sure that the ex con Stewart Colt was involved in some way to the rape cases. The toxicology reports would be coming in soon and it was highly likely that a semen match would be possible providing they could get him in for questioning. Now that was another thing all together.

'I've collected all the information available on Stewart Colt. I think you might be interested in the findings.' DI Barrow told Chrissie over the phone.

'I'll fax you all the details once I've had them typed up. I'm looking into a man called Stewart Pearce, he could be one and the same man. He was adopted and recently had contact with his older sister and a younger brother.'

'That sounds promising, well done. Who's working with you on this?' Chrissie asked.

'I've got DS Hartley, PC Campbell, DS Trivott and a couple of bobbies with me.'

'Ok, good luck with that, keep me informed.'

'I think we've finally got a breakthrough here, at least with the rape and murder case.' James told her.

'Yes, it's looking good. I'll be available via my mobile if you need to contact me. Great work, thank the gang for me will you.'

'Will do.' James told her as he hung up.

Chrissie checked the forensic pathology report. The cause of death in both the rape cases was due to a single stab wound to the heart. This had been expertly executed to cause death. The killer knew exactly where to place the weapon to pierce the heart. This killer knew how to do much more than just the act of killing. A dangerous man was on the loose and it was imperative that he was caught before he could commit any more heinous killings.

'Sally, could you ask Cheryl Teal if she can spare me a few moments this afternoon? I need to give her the details of this suspect and get some feedback. If she's too busy I'll have to work without her input.'

'No problem, I'll get back to you on that.'

Chrissie checked her mobile phone, there was a message from Janny.

'Meet me in the Halfpenny at lunchtime sugar lump. I've got info and want to share it with you. I've got a hell of a lot of lust too.

I'll be waiting for you around 1.30pm.

See you soon my lovely lollypop, can't wait to lick you later.'

'Love you.
Your lusty lover Jan xxxx'

Chrissie felt an instant flush of sexual arousal stir within her lower stomach. She sent a reply to Janny accepting the invitation.

Now she had work to do.

Cheryl had called in at the station on her way to a court case she was providing profiling evidence for. She didn't have long but she gave Chrissie a quick rundown of some relevant traits of the potential suspect Stewart Colt and promised a full report later.

The forensic team had been very busy collecting and checking samples and evidence from the various crime scenes. Chrissie had filled the incident boards with all the information they had gathered so far. Mary Childs in forensics had faxed her the reports as they had become available. Sonya Keats, Mildred Chalmers, Andrew MacDonald and David Haig had all contributed to the reports. They also had the newbie, David Harris now. He had already proven himself to be a very valuable member of the forensic team. Janny was pleased with the findings of all her team.

They had also been working on the disembodied hearts that had been delivered to Janny. They had all expected the same thing, that the hearts would most likely have come from the heartless victims. The tests results when they were returned, had proved to be as they had already expected.

All the hearts had matched up with the heartless

victims. All apart from one that is. The body that was missing the heart in question had not yet turned up. There was no doubt it would be discovered at some stage.

*

Previously

Terry Callum was shutting up shop when he decided that this evening he was going to do something different for a change. As a pharmacist he was very good. But he lacked the spark in his life that would lighten up his private life. It was ok to live and breathe work as long as there was something else to enjoy outside the work environment. He had decided to go to his local pub that evening, a place he didn't frequent very often. He did know most of the people who went there. He just didn't interact much once he had finished work. Sometimes he was just too tired to bother. At other times he felt slightly insecure and didn't want to have to talk to anyone. He had to be sociable in his line of work, so it wasn't that easy to carry it on once he had finished his working day.

'*Yes,*' He thought to himself.

'*I'll go straight to the pub tonight and have a drink and a bite to eat before returning home.*'

The range rover was slowing down as it approached Terry. He didn't notice it, he was too busy thinking about what he was going to do that evening. He hadn't noticed the person in the passenger seat get out. He vaguely noticed someone dressed in a coverall walk past him, and then he felt the sharp prick of the needle that had injected the debilitating substance into his neck. A look of terrified shock and bewilderment was sketched on Terry's face as he was escorted to the waiting car. He couldn't move very well, it was as though his body had ceased to work. That was all he could remember at that point in time. He would later realise he really wouldn't want to remember anything after that.

When he slowly came back to consciousness, it wasn't something that he would have wanted to come back to. He instinctively knew that he was going to die, and he knew he was going to die, in a most horrific way.

'Please,…….. God, help me.'

The surgeon was all scrubbed up and ready now. This was the final attempt, the last chance, then it would all be over. The clean up would have to take place afterwards, there wasn't much time left. Everything would have to be perfect for it to go right this time, there could be no more attempts after this.

34

In the Halfpenny pub, Ryan Guilder sat at the table hugging his pint of best bitter. Today he wanted beer, he had just found out that he had been shortlisted for a job at the Royal Infirmary Hospital. He had applied for a job as a porter there and was over the moon at being in the running for it. This was the best result that he'd had in an interview for a long time. He'd almost given up hope of ever being employed again. Now he had been given that hope.

'Hey up Chippy.' Ryan said as Chippy entered the pub.

'Hey up mate.' Chippy said as he approached the bar. He ordered a pint of lager and made his way to the table where he and his mates usually sat.

'How's it going?' Chippy asked him.

'I'm ok, in fact I'm very optimistic at the moment. Got a second interview for the job at the hospital.'

'Hey that's great mate.'

Just then Dougie Collins walked in and joined the friends. He ordered a pint of lager then he sat down gulping the first half of it down in one.

'Bloody shit day.' He told them when he came up for air.

'What happened?' Chippy asked him.

'Bloody middle aged woman wanted more than her boiler servicing and she looked like the back end of a fucking bus. Then, when I managed to get out of there intact, the next call was pretty much the same. What is it with these pathetic housewives eh? I mean I'm no oil painting, so what's the bloody attraction?'

'Well, chance would be a bloody fine thing with me, I haven't had an offer like that in years. And there you are getting em left right and bloody centre.' Ryan told him.

'I'm happily married, I don't need this shit.'

'Well just think yourself lucky then.' Chippy told him.

The friends were enjoying a pub lunch and a couple of pints together as they usually do when they get the chance. The topic of conversation soon came around to the murder investigations.

'It's getting past a joke now. How many bodies have there been discovered over the last few weeks or so? Quite a few to my reckoning. The police should have caught up with someone by now don't you think?' Chippy said.

Ryan finished off his pint.

'I just hope they don't give some poor innocent guy the run-around like they did with me.' He cringed slightly when he recalled being arrested for a murder he hadn't committed in the stamp master case.

'Surely that wouldn't happen again, not after last time. The cops should have learnt from their past mistakes. Plus you don't fit the criteria this time. Not unless you've taken a crash course in heart surgery.' Dougie laughed.

'Well, they'd better get their fingers out because this murderer is on a roll. The last two murders were different. Apparently, they were women and they had been raped and mutilated before being stabbed.'

'It's like Deja vu, we've certainly been here before haven't we. I wonder why our locality has been affected by multiple serial killers. Must be something in the water eh. Anyways, I'm off now, see you all soon.' Dougie told them. 'Bye you lot, its back to the grindstone again for me now.'

*

Terry Callum could see that he was in an operating theatre but it was like something from a horror movie. It was an old building with old fashioned operating facilities. This must be a bad dream he thought initially. He soon became aware that this was no dream, just a waking nightmare. He was petrified, he knew there was no hope. No one would find him here, he was doomed to this fate.

Whatever that was, he knew it wasn't good and he knew he was as good as dead right now.

Janny had been in there with him in her dream, she had seen his anguish and felt some of his fear and pain. It wasn't nice to have to witness these murders without being able to help the victims. She was still a novice, surely there must be some way to be able to stop these crimes from happening. At the moment though all Janny had was the dreams. She didn't know if they would be helpful or not. She hoped that they would be. In her dream she could see the surgeon preparing for the operation. Janny wished she could call the police and help him. It wasn't as if she knew it was happening in real time. This dream could be of something that has already taken place. She had to try and decipher where this place was. It was their only chance to find the murderer and if they could find this location it would provide plenty of forensic evidence. She thought deeply about the dream. The clues were all in the dreams, she just had to know how to interpret them.

She was on a learning curve, but she was determined to tap into them. She would have to try and find out what they meant. It maybe that she would never know why she was having them, but for now she needed to be aware of everything the dreams were showing her.

*

Chrissie's phone rang.

It was DS Hartley.

'We've got some information on the second rape-murder case. She's been identified as Tanya Colleen, aged thirty two. Worked as a lap dancer at a club in Drayfield. We're checking through her details, but I thought you'd want to know who the woman is right now. I'll let you have a report of the full details as soon as it's been typed up.'

'Thanks for that, I really need to find a link between the two murders and we'll need to interview her work mates and any next of kin need to be informed. Can I leave you and DI Barrow to deal with that?'

'Yes, I'll arrange to get that sorted. I'll let you know as soon as I have anything to report.'

35

Stewart Colt had given up on Alex, it was sad but hell he didn't even know him. Tough, because life is tough. He had his own life to live. Plus it was only a matter of time before he would be discovered. Now was the time to get away before he was arrested for the murder of the two women. He had been busy planning this, but first maybe just one final victim could be fitted in. He smiled to himself.

*

Pippa Downing was nearing the end of her shift as a waitress in the restaurant. She was looking forward to unwinding in a long hot bath and then chilling in front of the TV. Her evening was planned out, she would send out for a take away and open a bottle of wine to wash it down.

She had just waited on a man who was dining on his own. This would probably be her last order of the night. She would serve him and then get herself ready to leave.

'Would you like a drink?' The man asked her.

'Sorry, I can't drink while I'm working, but thank you for offering.'

Pippa could feel the man watching her, it was

kind of creepy, but she was going home soon so he could go and take a running jump as far as she was concerned.

The man had already finished his meal and had asked for a refill of coffee which he drank before leaving the restaurant. It was a very close evening hot and humid, the man waited outside for the waitress to appear.

Pippa changed into her home clothes and collected her things before leaving. She was flagging now and in need of the bath she had promised herself.

As she left the restaurant she saw the man she had recently served. He was standing on the corner and watching Pippa as she walked through the car park. She was going to walk home, it would only take a few minutes to reach her flat.

Pippa pretended not to notice the man as she headed towards the car park exit towards the road.

She could see out of the corner of her eye that the man was approaching her.

'I really can't be doing with this.' Pippa thought.

'Hey there, would you like to join me for that drink now? It would help you to unwind after a hard day at work.' The man asked her.

'Thanks for the offer, but I'm really too tired. I just want to go home to have a nice hot bath and relax. Sorry. But thank you all the same.'

'Ok, no problem. Maybe some other time eh?'

'Yeah.'

Pippa set off towards the road. She could see the man was still following her. This was not good. She walked a bit quicker. The sooner she reached the road the safer she would feel.

'Hey there, how about I give you a lift home instead. Straight home no strings.'

'No thanks, I don't need a lift, its not far and I like to walk. I know you mean well but I would rather just walk home.'

'Ok, if that's what you want.'

The man approached Pippa and as they reached his car he opened the passenger door and grabbed Pippa. He punched her in the stomach which knocked the wind out of her. He bundled her in his car and drove off with a stunned and frightened Pippa as his captive passenger.

He drove to a secluded spot then brutally raped her. He drove his fist into her face and body as he forced himself upon her. Pippa tried to scream but her throat was filling up with blood and choking her.

'You are mine now bitch. I'm going to rape the arse of you and make you beg me to kill you. You are so lucky slut, you get to be fucked before you die.' He told her as he worked on her face some more.

She looked a bloody mess, her teeth were

smashed and her mouth couldn't be recognised her whole face was covered in blood and broken.

Pippa could do nothing to stop him. She was at his mercy. God help her, he was in control and he wasn't going to let her live. She knew that.

The knife pierced her heart with a precise incision and as Pippa was bleeding out, her life ebbed away with it.

Pippa was dumped by the roadside just like the others had been.

*

The night before Pippa Downing was killed, Janny had dreamed of the murder. She had told Chrissie who had made some notes. The dream had shown Janny a young woman in her twenties who worked in a restaurant. Janny had seen her in her uniform. She saw a man who was in the restaurant. He was the murderer. She also saw the rape and brutality, which was horrific. She then witnessed the final act of the knife entering her heart. Janny described the man as clearly as she could so that Chrissie could compare the description with any suspects

36

Chrissie had just received the information she was waiting for on Stewart Colt as James had promised. It appeared he was born Stewart Pearce. He was adopted and renamed Stewart Colt.

He had a sister and a younger brother who were both adopted they all went to different families. Stewart hadn't had the same opportunities as his sister and brother. Although he had been gifted with being able to retain massive amounts of information, which enabled him to quickly understand medical terminology. He was no way in the same league as his sister and brother.

His sister had been adopted by a wealthy family and was apparently an expert in her field. She was lucky enough to have been placed with parents who had put her through university and medical school. She excelled to the highest degree in her field.

The youngest brother had excelled in mathematics and was bordering on genius. He had been diagnosed with heart disease and was placed on the waiting list for a heart transplant.

Their birth parents had both been drug addicts. When the children had been born there had been some undetected drug related damage to all the three children. It was a while before the authorities had picked up on this. The parents had at some point overdosed on drugs and both died.

The children were taken into care. Both their

parents had shown some psychotic tendencies which had probably been passed down to the children. A lot of damage had been done to the children that had gone unnoticed. All of the children had shown some child prodigy tendencies which had possibly missed a few generations.

Chrissie was convinced that Stewart Colt or a.k.a. Stewart Pearce was the culprit in the rape and murder cases. She wanted him in for questioning a.s.a.p.

He fitted the description Janny had provided from her premonitions and Cheryl Teal had built up a good profile for the killer which also matched up with Stewart's background. She knew she would have to make sure she had everything in place before making an arrest but the odds were stacking against Stewart. He was their man, she had no doubt about that.

They already had a DNA sample on file for Stewart, so it was just a case of getting a match. The forensic team were working on that right now. It was only a matter of time before they had him.

Chrissie knew that there was a significant motive for the heartless murders in the family too. She was going to look into that. That would definitely be her next move.

Janny had sent a Chrissie a text. A lovely sexy one. It was nice to get back to how they used to be. They were getting back on track which was how it should be. Chrissie looked at her phone which was on vibrate and smiled. She was so happy to have things sorted between her and Janny. She really appreciated their relationship now more than anything else. Even the murders didn't seem to be stressing her out as much now, knowing that Janny would always be there for her.

Her smile soon faded when she received a call from the desk sergeant on duty John Baker.

'The body of a young woman has been discovered by the roadside between Hairdale and Lockington. DI Barrow and DS Hartley are on their way to the scene now. The first response team is cordoning off the area and forensics are on their way.'

'Ok thanks Sergeant Baker. Can you get me a car and driver to take me there?'

'Yes Ma'am, I'll do that right now and let you know when it's ready.'

'Thanks.'

Well that's Janny's premonition verified.' She thought.

Janny had been informed, she had already set off to the crime scene along with the forensic team.

'Oh no, here we go again.' Janny thought.

Janny noticed as soon as she arrived at the scene, that this was exactly like she had seen it in her special dreams. The victim was a young woman who appeared to be in her twenties. The woman's hair was a dark auburn shade of red. After taking a quick look at her, it was obvious she had been beaten and raped. Just like the other rape murder victims this woman had been stabbed in the heart.

Chrissie arrived at the scene and talked with the responding officers. Then she had a word with DI

Barrow and DS Hartley. It was apparent that the same person that had murdered the previous two women killed this latest victim. Chrissie was convinced that it was Stewart Colt who had committed the murders of the three women.

The forensic team were busy collecting trace evidence and photographic evidence of the area. Anything that was deemed to be important was being collected. Items were documented, listed, dated, bagged up and signed out by the person who had collected them. Janny was doing a quick check of the body to estimate the, time of death.

In the previous rape murder cases, the killer didn't wait very long before ditching the victim's bodies. It appeared to be the same in this case.

Janny would be escorting the body back to the morgue when it was ready to be moved.

37

That evening Chrissie and Janny were drinking wine and chillaxing together. It had been a stressful, but also a productive day. They had gone home straight from work so they could spend some quality time together, reflecting on what the day had brought.

'Well we can't say we're bored. I'm convinced the rape and murders were committed by Stewart Colt. He's also known as Stewart Pearce.' Chrissie told Janny.

'Whatever happens, you'll need to bring him in for questioning. I don't think he'll be making himself readily available somehow.'

'I just hope I haven't left it too late. It's taken me long enough to put two and two together. I realized eventually, that it was more than likely to be someone who had been disgruntled and let down by the system. Cheryl's profile of the rape killer fitted Stewart Colt-Pearce. I just wish I'd noticed much sooner. Instead, I decided to try and break up our relationship like a proper idiotic moron. I was concentrating more on analysing you and myself. I'd risked everything we had once had together. I am so very sorry Janny. You didn't deserve that.'

'It's all water under the bridge, I'm sure you'll eventually come across the vital clues and evidence you need to tie him to the victims. I'll do everything I can to help you.'

'Only time will tell.' Chrissie whispered.

Janny gave Chrissie a quick rundown of the findings she had discovered during her investigations earlier. The post-mortem had been performed as soon as Janny had returned with the body.

It was nice that now they could relax and reflect on their day, just like they used to do. Soon they settled down to enjoy their evening together. They watched some TV and opened a bottle of wine. It was proving to be a very nice ending to what had been a harrowing day.

The two women were contented together, they had seemingly managed to put away most of their differences. They were working together to fill in the delicate cracks that had appeared in their relationship. Despite all the upset, they were beginning to get their lives back on track. For Chrissie and Janny, this was now the start of the rest of their lives together. This time they knew what was what. No more stupid accusations or doubts about what their relationship had been before. It had evolved into what they had now. They were sound.

Once the two women had showered they felt more relaxed. They made love in a slow, sensitive and loving way. Then they sent out for a Chinese take away. The meal was very nice, and they had both enjoyed it. Still drinking the wine, they had opted to watch a DVD before retiring to bed.

They slept together that night in a deep and fitful sleep. That would hopefully refresh them both for whatever horrors tomorrow might bring.

38

Chrissie was at her desk when the phone rang. It was DI Barrow.

'We now know who the victim is. Pippa Downing, she worked as a waitress in a restaurant. A twenty seven year old single woman. Auburn hair, slim build and she had finished her last shift at the restaurant last night. We've checked out the CCTV footage. It looks out onto the car park of the restaurant and there is some footage of her talking to a man who incidentally fits the description of Stewart Colt. There's a DNA check on going to identify him as being at the scene of the murder. We found a few stray hairs that weren't Pippa Downing's. We're expecting it could be a match to Stewarts DNA.'

'Great stuff James, well done. What was the name of the restaurant?'

'The restaurant is in Drayfield. It's called 'The Woodsman' part of the Wetherspoon's chain. The CCTV footage was quite clear so we should be able to get an admissible ID on Stewart Colt.'

'Great, right, we need to get a squad out to arrest Stewart at his last known address. He's still on parole so it shouldn't be too difficult to get some info on his activities since he was released from prison. We also need to get some information on his blood relatives, apparently his siblings were all adopted separately. We need to know who his blood siblings are as soon as possible.'

'We're already onto it. I'll be in touch when we have more details.'

'That's brilliant James. Keep me in the loop.'

Chrissie had no sooner finished talking with DI Barrow when her phone rang again. It was Cheryl Teal the criminal psychologist.

'I thought you might like a quick profile on the latest murder. God it's getting bloody rife with victims at the moment isn't it. Good luck to you in catching the murderer. By the looks of it, you're going to need it. The person who killed the last victim, is in my opinion the same person who committed the other two previous murders. I would safely say that this person fits the description of Stewart Colt who you asked me to look into. I've looked into his past records and activities since he left prison. He has a placement at the Special Heart Unit a private hospital somewhere in Drayfield. His sister works there too, I haven't been able to identify who it is though. The records are very sketchy.'

'Thanks for that Cheryl. I've got your details about the Heartless murders in front of me now and it doesn't look as though it could be the same person. That doesn't mean he's not involved in some way though. I'm going to bring Stewart Colt in for questioning, so hopefully that will prove to be constructive. Hopefully the test results will be a match when they come in, this will seal his guilt. Then we will be able to remove a rapist and murderer from the streets.'

Within a few minutes Chrissie's phone rang again.

'It's like a bloody hot line' she thought.

It was the police commissioner David Maroni wanting to know what was happening.

Chrissie informed him of the pending arrest of Stewart Colt and that seemed to calm him down a bit but he was still out for blood on the other murders.

It was very busy in the police headquarters with people coming and going. Officers were reporting in and writing out reports, then going out again. Detectives were in and out of the offices. So far so good Chrissie thought.

Extra homicide detectives had been called in to help with the footwork. Teams were often seconded if a major incident occurred, to provide extra manpower. Quite often the teams would interact. They would eventually get to know officers from other areas. Many knew each other from previous secondments.

*

The surgeon was agitated, the equipment wasn't up to date and the patient was very weak. The life of the patient depended on what resources were available and right now the odds were stacked against him.

This last donor was a perfect match, this one had to be spot on, and it was the last chance. The surgeon knew there would be no more opportunities after this one last final attempt. The police were rapidly becoming aware of what was happening, it was only a matter of time before everything went pear shaped.

The nurse was getting more and more agitated and she would end up rebelling against the surgeon, it didn't help that she was being sexually abused. Things were getting to be very dangerous now. The surgeon sighed and scrubbed up, ready to check on the patient. Everything depended on what happens next.

Earlier attempts when performing the heart transplant's had been unsuccessful and now those bodies were turning up one after the other. This was inevitable but the surgeon knew that this was the beginning of the end…

The surgeon was also aware of an intruder squatting in the old hospital. This was another thorn to contend with, something else to decide what to do about it. This will all have to be investigated at some point. Right now the main concern was for the patient. Then the other loose ends could be sorted out as and when required. The surgeon didn't think anything was more important than saving the patient. The patient had been waiting so long for the heart that should have been given to him in the first place. If that hadn't been the case none of these measures would have had to take place. The surgeon sighed a deep and heavy almost defeated sigh.

'*This will never do,*' the surgeon thought, '*I must stay positive….*"

Sex was great with the young nurse, this was something the surgeon would miss the most.

It was time to finish what had been started, it was time to transplant the heart into the patient. Once that was completed, the surgeon would have to tidy up the mess and cover up all traces of them being there. Making sure there were no incriminating tracks for the police to follow. It would probably mean a few deaths along the way. Nothing could be left that would tie the surgeon to any of the operations.

This was the final hurdle and it would need to be performed perfectly in order for them to remain undiscovered. A forward plan had been prepared, ready to put into place when it was necessary. It was almost necessary.

The surgeon was angry with the assistant. He was over stretching the mark and putting everything at risk. He had committed the rape and murder of some women. This was stupid, why on earth would he want to put the whole project at risk? Nothing could condone what he had done. It would only be a matter of time before the police put two and two together. Then to top it off he had sent some hearts to Dr Stowers that could possibly tie them to the heartless murders. He was becoming a bloody joke and a liability.

Stewart Colt was angry at being got at. He had done everything his sister had wanted him to do. It was his turn now to have some fun. Who the hell did she think she was? She was a bloody lesbian anyway;

she could do with a good man shag. That would put her right, the silly bitch. They had done everything they could to try and save their brother Alex Wilson. He was their younger brother so they had felt responsible for him once they had found him again. They had all been adopted and brought up by different adoptive parents. They had all had completely different upbringings. His sister had been adopted by rich parents and so had his younger brother Alex.

She had helped her brother Alex Wilson as much as she could once she had found him again. It wasn't enough though, she couldn't get him a heart transplant. He had to go through the usual channels there was nothing she could do. That was until she had taken matters into her own hands. The whole thing had just escalated from there. There was no going back from this if she was caught. After all the planning and the operations, it had all been for nothing. She just didn't have enough help or equipment for the conditions to be right. It had all been a waste of time, the last and final operation had failed in the end, and that was it now. There was nothing more she could do for her younger brother Alex. He was only twenty nine, she felt so inadequate because she had not been able to help him. She had lost it. It had driven her to lose her sanity with the overwhelming obsession to save him.

Stewart on the other hand hadn't had the same opportunities and he had ended up straying from the beaten track, on a number of occasions.

39

Mary was becoming more and more agitated as the day progressed. She was listening intently to the voices, they were telling her to stay where she was for now. They warned her that there would be a higher risk of her getting caught if she were to venture outside. Mary heeded the voices, she had always trusted their judgement for her safety. That didn't help her at the moment, because she was becoming frightened of this place. She had felt safe when she'd first arrived there, but now she didn't feel safe anymore. There was someone else in the building and she didn't want whoever it was to find her cosy home. She was aware that any noise she made now would be detrimental to her safety. The voices agreed with her.

Mary was feeling hungry so she decided to leave the building and brave the pub, at least she would be relatively safe in there. Providing she didn't draw attention to herself that is. The voices agreed.

It was cosy in the pub, Mary had ordered pie, chips and peas for her lunch, with gravy. She was sipping her hot coffee as the meal arrived. It was a real luxury to have a hot meal now that she was free from the institution. This was quite civilised, she could get used to this. For the first time in a while Mary felt contented again. The voices were quiet at the moment. It was pleasantly pleasing, to be able to listen to the soft relaxing music that was being piped through the speakers. As she ate her lunch, Mary thought about what she was going to do about her home. She realised that she would probably have to leave what had been initially her safe haven. The thought of having to look for another place to stay was daunting. She would have preferred to stay where she was.

As the afternoon progressed, Mary was aware that she would soon have to return to the old building. The thought of this was making her feel more and more distressed. She had to make a move soon, she'd been sitting in the pub much longer than she had intended. The voices agreed.

40

They met up for lunch in Jack's café. Chrissie and Janny exchanged information regarding the latest rape victim Pippa Downing. They were eating sandwiches and drinking ice cold diet coke. It was stifling outside, the sun was blazing down. They were still in the middle of a heatwave at the moment.

Having finished their lunches, the two women were about to return to work. Janny had started to make rude suggestions to Chrissie.

'Chrissie, I'm a very randy girl. Have we got time for a quickie in the loo eh?'

'Sorry darling, you'll have to wait until later, just you wait until I get you home. I'm going to have to frisk you.' Chrissie said.

'Ohh, promises, promises. I can't wait. Did you say frisk or fuck? Why don't we go straight home tonight and get a takeaway. It will save us time and we can utilise that time to do more interesting things after eating. We've got a few bottles of wine left at mine if you want to come and help me drink a few glasses.'

'Sounds good to me.'

Chrissie checked her mobile phone. There

hadn't been any messages or missed calls. She felt worn out, it would be nice to be able to relax with Janny later. With that in mind she returned to work.

There were piles of reports on her desk they had been delivered or faxed while she had been out having her lunch. She fingered through the paperwork, quickly scanning the contents for anything that might be important.

The tox reports had arrived confirming the drugs that had been used in the kidnapping cases. Chrissie had already put the results on the whiteboard.

This was a real challenge but Chrissie was feeling confident now. She was getting her mojo back. *'Bring it on.'* She thought to herself.

*

Chrissie had been so upset following the incident with Janny. Her behaviour had been uncalled for and irrational. She knew it wasn't normal, there was no way she would have reacted in that way under normal circumstances. It had shocked her into ringing her psychiatrist Carol Higgins. She had made an appointment and attended it even though she didn't really have the time, she had made the time. This was important in her work and especially in her relationship with Janny.

Carol was a very good listener. Chrissie poured her heart out to her and had felt a huge release following her explanation of what had happened.

'Because of the trauma you suffered when you thought Janny was going to die. Then the relief you felt when you knew that she was going to live. All those pent up emotions have created a fear inside you that makes you afraid you will lose her again. You are so afraid of losing her that your mind is creating false scenarios tricking you into imagining all sorts of unfounded and irrational thoughts and feelings you wouldn't normally have.'

'I can't believe I actually thought Janny was a suspect in the murder case. It's so far from the truth its bordering on stupid personified.' Chrissie told her.

'Once Janny gets over the hurt she felt at the time, she will realise what is causing your irrational behaviour. Janny has her own demons to fight too. You are both deeply affected by what happened during that investigation. You can help each other get through this, but you have to face up to what happened and not let it rule your present lives. Together you will be strong and you will be able to support each other.'

'You are right of course, and I feel much better for having talked to you about it. Thank you for listening.'

'No problem Chrissie, it's my job. I know you've got a lot on at the moment, but I really think it would help if you could book a few appointments here so I can monitor how things are panning out with you. I think you are on the mend, but it will take time.'

Chrissie agreed to this and felt much better for having had the consultation with Carol. She didn't feel so bad about herself now. It was up to her to try and take back control over her life and more importantly her thoughts.

*

That evening the two women chilled out together by having a shower, sending for a take away, drinking some fine wine and making mad passionate love.

'I love you Chrissie Charles, you know that don't you? I couldn't imagine my life without you darling. We are so very lucky to have each other. We should never ever take each other for granted. Our lives are not our own they belong with each other. Never forget that, never ever doubt the love we share. We are true soul mates and have been truly blessed by the powers that be. We were meant to be together forever.'

'Janny, I love you more than life itself. I admit that I had a few moments of deranged stupidity probably brought on by stress. I really never meant to hurt you. I can't believe that I actually did. There are no excuses, I know how lucky I am. I'm so glad that you have stood by me and forgiven me for what was an unforgivable attack on you.'
The two women retired to bed that evening very much in love with each other and definitely back to how they had been before. It was a major breakthrough for their relationship. This was a golden moment and one that would last them forever. Or while ever they were both alive. They say that love goes on even after death, but it's the here and now that counts. They knew that they should live

each moment as if it was their last. To always enjoy every minute, even in bad situations. Together they were a team, together they were strong. Together they could conquer anything, they just had to stay together.

41

Janny had dreamed about another heartless victim. She tried to remember as many details as possible. She wrote the main details down onto a notepad that she had now taken to keeping on the bedside cabinet. She would show Chrissie what she had written in the morning. It was much better now that Chrissie had accepted her premonitions as a fact rather than a fantasy. The facts that had emerged from her dreams could not be ignored.

The following morning it was business as usual, following an early morning chat over breakfast. Janny told Chrissie about her dream and gave her the notes she had made during the night. Chrissie thanked her and they both went their separate ways. The day was already beginning to warm up. The forecast had said it was going to be another red hot, sticky and humid day.

'Nice weather if you don't have to work in it. Definitely not ideal conditions for trying to solve murder cases.' DCI Chrissie Charles thought to herself.

Chrissie could feel the heat rising inside her, this was making her feel uncomfortable. Already she could feel the sweat threatening to expose itself.

'This is a great start to the working day. I really must calm down and stay cool before the sun comes out to scorch the

life out of us all.' Chrissie thought.

*

PC Amy Campbell had been following her own leads. She wanted to do a good job in order to redeem herself in her position as a police officer. She had made things very difficult for herself and now she felt obliged to try and make things right. She knew that DCI Charles had been very lenient with her, so she wanted to help as much as she could. She wanted to prove herself worthy of being part of the team.

DI Barrow had gone in to work very early, he wanted to get a good start on things before the heat made it almost unbearable to even think. He wasn't at the station long before DS Hartley and DS Trivett turned up. Everyone had the same idea. Get cracking before it gets too hot. The sun was already rising and burning off the early morning mist. Shining down between the few clouds that did not really provide much of a shield against the sun's rays.

Mike winked at Sharon as they entered the incident room. There was time for a quick chat and a coffee before the morning briefing. James studied the whiteboard as he sipped his wet, weak and barely warm coffee.

The desk sergeant had just arrived to take over from the evening shift. John Baker helped himself to a coffee before settling in behind the counter in the reception area.

'Phew, its bloody hot already, I'll be glad when this heatwave is over. It doesn't suit me when it's this hot. You can put layers of clothes on if it's cold but you're limited as to what you can remove.' Sergeant Baker said as he settled himself into his reception booth. He switched on the desk fan it was already very warm.

The early morning shift was beginning to arrive in dribs and drabs. All the officers were complaining about the heatwave. Most of them were complaining that they hadn't had much sleep because it had been too uncomfortable in bed. Even with windows open and fans blowing, the heat was still there well into the night. Sleep wasn't easy and most of the staff were still tired.

In the incident room, the officers gathered ready for DCI Charles' arrival. They were going over their caseloads and preparing for the day ahead of them. Not an easy one in this heat. There was something about the heat that tended to addle the brain. Judgements and thoughts were not as clear as they would have been. They could all end up with cotton wool for brains, once the humid and sweaty heat of the day set in.

Chrissie arrived earlier than usual and was greeted by Sally who brought in her morning coffee.

'Good morning Sally, thank you. I hope you managed to get some sleep last night. It was very hot again wasn't it? I was very tired, which helped, I did manage to sleep at least some of the night.'

'I found it very hot and sticky, but I managed to get in a few hours sleep. I had a tower fan on in the bedroom. I left it on all night. The only trouble was, it ended up circulating warm air. It was better than nothing I suppose.' Sally replied.

Chrissie noticed that Sally wasn't quite her usual bubbly self. This heat was affecting everyone.

Once the briefing was over, the officers went on to do their shifts. Chrissie looked at her phone, there hadn't been any messages as yet. She checked her emails and replied to as many as she could before she started to work on the murder cases.

It was vital to the investigation that they find Stewart Colt. He was now DCI Charles' most wanted suspect in the rape murders. The heartless murders were still a mystery, Chrissie had assigned teams of officers to follow up on the leads they had acquired so far. The heartless murderer was still out there, a medically trained person who at the moment was undetectable.

Chrissie was perusing through some of the reports on her desk when the phone rang. It was DI Barrow.

'We've got another body. A man in his forties found in a skip outside a restaurant in Haddonfield. He has an operation scar on his chest like the other heartless victims. I've already alerted the forensic team and the first response team are there cordoning the area off.'

'Not another one, it's getting past a fucking joke now. We've got body's coming out of our sodding earholes, I'm on my way, give me the directions.'

The first response team had put up a cordon around the area where the body was discovered. The road had been blocked off by parking police vehicles across the road. Police officers were questioning any vehicle as they approached the crime scene.

The squad car with DCI Chrissie Charles on board pulled up just as the forensic team arrived. Janny was already there with David Harris, they were looking at the body and making notes before the forensic work began. They had no doubt that this was the work of the heartless killer, it had all the same features as the other cases.

'How much are you betting that this victim is a match for the unidentified heart in the lab?' Janny said to Chrissie as she was getting into her coverall suit.

'This is getting ridiculous, we must catch this fucking surgeon before it happens again. I can't believe how many bodies' we've got piled up in the morgue. What with the heartless victims and the rape and murder victims we have a grand total of seven body's, seven bloody bodies.' Chrissie stated.

42

The body that had been discovered was that of Terry Callum, he was forty five years old and had dark thinning hair. He had worked as a pharmacist at a Boot's chemist in Lockington for over three years. He lived in Haddonfield which is about five miles from Lockington. He was single and lived alone.

Apparently he hadn't been seen since leaving work. The staff who worked at Boot's had tried to contact him unsuccessfully and reported him missing to the police. They were concerned because it was unusual for Terry Callum not to attend work. On the very few rare occasions he hadn't gone into work he would always let the shop know. Terry knew they would have to get a locum pharmacist in to cover for him.

Following the discovery of Terry Callum's body, the forensic team checked out the crime scene. His body had been discovered in a skip outside a restaurant in Drayford. Janny had helped to collect trace samples along with the forensic team that were attending. The smell was horrendous and it seemed like millions of flies were being drawn to the lifeless body that had been dumped in the skip. They had sent many samples onto the lab. The police photographers had collected numerous photo shots and some video footage of the scene.

In the incident room information was building up on the white boards. The room had been taken over with the extra whiteboards that held relevant information on all the seven victims. On one of the boards with all the other victims, was a recent photograph of Terry Callum, it was as he had looked before he was killed. There were other various photographs of the crime scene, including some graphic pictures of the body after death.

Janny did the post mortem once the body had been moved to the morgue. During the post-mortem Janny reported that the body of Terry Callum appeared to be just like the other heartless murder cases. The heart had been surgically removed during what had appeared to be an attempt at a heart transplant operation, but the heart had not been replaced. It could have been that the heart had been removed from this donor to go into a person who was in urgent need of a new heart. If that was the case, whoever was doing this had to have had quite an extensive knowledge on the subject. This in itself narrowed down the suspects. It was a highly skilled occupation in which case it should be relatively easy to get a list of specialised surgeons. This is a good positive turning point in the investigation. This victim was going to help them by providing more clues. When Janny eventually received the results of the DNA test, it was as she had expected. The final heart that had been in the package delivered to Dr Janny Stowers, had belonged to the body of Terry Callum.

*

That evening Janny and Chrissie reflected on the recent events and results of some of the tests. They

224

were eating their evening meal in the Travellers Rest a pub and restaurant in Sheffield's town centre. It was one of their favourite haunts. The pub had great food, dimmed lighting and piped music which created a cosy and warm ambience. The open fire would be lit in the winter, but with it being summer it wasn't needed. Especially in this heat wave which seemed to be lasting forever, very unusual. There was no sign of a let up yet.

'I was talking with Cheryl Teal earlier, she was explaining how the heartless murder profile fits in with other serial killers profiles.' Chrissie told Janny.

'She told me that in most cases, serial killers tended to plan and then execute murders. They also tend to name themselves, for example Jack the Ripper. They plan the murders for a long time and intend to carry on for a long time. In the heartless murders, this doesn't appear to be the case. She informed me that the killer in this case is most likely trying to save someone. In order to do this, the killer has had to either kill the victims or they've died during the operations. It appears that whatever the killer had initially planned hadn't worked out in the way it was intended. So it has carried on.'

'I've completed the post mortem report and included the results of the unidentified heart DNA test. No surprise that it's a positive match to Terry Callum. There are a few factors that could be significant to the overall investigation into the murders. I think that there's common denominator as to why the hearts were removed. Like Cheryl said, it could be that the killer was trying to save someone. The killer is in my opinion a highly skilled surgeon, so theoretically it should be much easier to track down a list of them. I would of course be one of the listed surgeons. There aren't all that many highly trained specialists in this area, so we should be able to create a shortlist of potential suspects.' Janny told her.

The two women returned home and shared a couple of bottles of red wine before retiring to bed. The wine at least helped them to relax before the stress of the next working day. After making love which left them feeling hot and sticky, they showered then attempted to sleep. Tossing and turning for what seemed like hours, the two women drifted in and out of a restless sleep. The electric fan was left on all night. It was very hot and sticky and even with the fan on they were uncomfortable. Lying on top of the covers naked, they tried not cuddle up, it was far too hot. If the two women had engaged in any naked flesh contact, they would probably have ended up stuck to each other.

43

Janny had another dream that night. It was a really vivid dream. She realised that she was involved in the dream much more than usual.

This is a vital clue, but what does it mean?' She thought.

In the dream she could see herself interacting with the surgeon. She had a strange thought that she might actually know this person, if so, she would probably know who the murder was. Or did she? It was either a premonition or just her mind playing games with her because of the heat. She wished she could control this special gift she had been given. It would be so much easier to determine what the dreams meant. She made a mental note to herself, to try and find out if this strange phenomenon could possibly be controlled to her advantage.

She wrote all the details down when she woke up just to clarify all the details before they faded. This done, she decided that tomorrow she would follow up on any of the leads provided from the dream. It was a clear dream but it was also food for thought. Something about the place sprang to mind when she relived the dream. She had a feeling that she knew the place. This was a good lead and she would have to follow it up. Chrissie would need to know the details, but she would be fine to go and visit the place.

She had to make sure that Chrissie was aware of her intensions. It was just a precaution, but she had promised her that she wouldn't do anything without her knowing. That decided, Janny tried to settle back into sleep. It was very hot and sticky, but eventually she had managed to nod off into a restless sleep.

The electric fan that was on in the bedroom didn't really help all that much, because the air that was being circulated was warm. A slight buzzing emitted from the tower fan creating a soothing ambient noise. The breeze from the fan was creating a draft which to some extent helped to keep the two women cool.

The women slept restlessly, tossing and turning well into the night. Janny dreamed again, but this time it was a normal dream. She knew instinctively that this dream wasn't a premonition. So now at least she had learned to recognise the difference between the two kinds of dreams. The ordinary dreams were just that. The premonition dreams were of a totally different nature. She could tell which was which now, she had learnt how to differentiate between the dreams so that had improved her control to some extent. Hopefully, her understanding of the gift she possessed would improve over time.

Chrissie stirred in her sleep and turned over, almost pushing Janny off the bed. Janny slowly moved Chrissie back over again to leave herself some space. Then she slid off the bed to go to the loo. On her return she carefully manoeuvred herself back onto the bed, taking care not to disturb Chrissie. As Janny tried to resume her restless sleep, the low buzzing of the fan helped to clear her mind. Thus closing down the many wayward thoughts that were jangling around in her head. The gentle buzzing of the fan was like listening to a white noise, which had created a similar effect. It wasn't too long before Janny nodded off again.

As the dawn broke, and the new day began, the birds sang their musical chorus. It was wake up time.

Chrissie and Janny had a quick breakfast before setting off to work. They were both blissfully unaware of what this new day would bring them.

*

Chrissie went to work and updated the incident board with information she had received about the latest murder victim Terry Callum. He was aged forty five, a pharmacist who worked at a branch of Boots chemist. He lived alone in Haddonfield which was five miles away from Lockington. He had dark thinning hair which had begun to turn grey. Terry Callum hadn't been seen since leaving work a few days earlier. His work colleagues had reported him missing. It was unusual for him to miss work, he had always been a punctual person. Because he was single and lived alone, work had been his main priority. It was all he had.

The post mortem results and tox reports were all there on the board, along with pictures and the DNA. verification of the extra heart that had been delivered to Janny matching his body.

44

Mary decided to investigate the source of the noises she had heard previously. She'd found the old operating theatre and the two small side wards. One of the wards contained a patient. It had been set up as an intensive care unit. The other ward contained a captive woman. The woman was tethered by a chain that allowed her some freedom of movement. It allowed her to walk between the room, the toilet and sink. The voices were warning Mary to leave the building. She entered the room cautiously. The nurse looked up as she entered.

'Hi I'm Mary, who are you?'

'Please help me, get me help please. I'm being held captive here. I've been raped and I've had to assist in the operations that have been done here. I think the surgeon is going to kill me. Please you have to help me to escape.'

Mary moved slowly towards the nurse.

'Is there a key for that chain?' Mary asked her.

'Yes, the surgeon keeps the key in a drawer in the other side ward. It's in the second drawer down. It unlocks these handcuffs that are attached to the chain. Please, do it quickly, before the surgeon returns. We haven't got much time.'

Mary quickly found the key and fumbled to release the nurse from her shackles. Once she'd released the nurse, Mary led a fearful Gabby Fielding towards where her own make shift digs were. This was the quickest way to leave the building. They left by that exit.

When they had exited the building, Gabby gave out an audible sigh of relief. Mary's voices were telling her to get the hell out of there as quickly as possible. Mary had already decided that she would need to return to her room to pick up her few personal belongings. They were hers and they were all she had in this world at the moment. She didn't want to leave her stuff in there. With her mind made up the voices subsided for a while, there was no point in trying to change her mind once it had been made up.

'I'm going back inside to get my belongings. You go and get help and explain what's happened here. Be careful not to let the surgeon see you if he returns.'

'Nooo, don't go back inside, it's dangerous in there, what if the surgeon comes back? You wouldn't stand a chance. Please, you've got to come with me and escape while you can. Nothing can be that important that you would want to put your life at risk for it. Please, come with me, I owe you my life, let me have the chance to repay you in some way. Come with me now.' Gabby pleaded with her.

'Don't you go worrying about me, I can take care of myself. This is my home and I am going to have to leave here now. So, I want to collect the few things that I own to take with me. Don't hang about here, go and get help. You're very young, you have your whole life ahead of you. Go and get on with the rest of your life. I hope it's a good one.'

'I wish you would come with me. It's not safe for you in there. Please reconsider and escape with me while you still can.'

'Go, leave me be, hurry while the coast is clear. Get some help and then all will be fine.' Mary said as she headed back through the entrance they had just exited from.

Gabby didn't follow her, she was too afraid. She set off at a rapid pace down the drive, towards the exit of the old hospital. Once she had left the premises, she ran as fast as she could towards the nearest building, which happened to be a shop. Gabby rushed inside and pleaded with the shop keeper, who was both shocked and surprised at the sudden dramatic entrance of the dishevelled woman.

'Please help me, call the police.' Gabby blurted out almost incoherently.

The shop keeper immediately rang the police thinking to herself, that whatever the reason this distraught woman wanted her to contact the police, it would no doubt merit the call.

While they were waiting for the police to arrive, the shopkeeper put the kettle on. Sweet strong tea was in order to combat the shock, she would make one for herself too.

The nurse began to blurt out her story to the shopkeeper, explaining what had happened to her. She sipped the sweet brown thick liquid. It tasted like syrup and wasn't that nice, but it was beginning to make her feel better. She started to feel much safer now.

'Don't worry, the police will be here soon. You'll be safe here. Look, I've shut up the shop so we won't be disturbed. It sounds like you've had a horrendous ordeal.'

'I thought I was going to die in there, I would have if it hadn't been for that wonderful woman who just happened to be squatting and living in the same building. I don't know who she is but I think she said her name was Mary. I wouldn't have stood a chance without her help. I'm frightened for her though. She insisted on returning for her belongings. I don't think she had many, but they meant so much to her. She was prepared to put them before her life.'

Within just over twenty minutes, the police arrived. They called an ambulance to take her to the hospital so she could be checked out. They called it in.

45

It was quite warm outside already, even though it was very early in the morning. The sky was blue and a few clouds were encroaching on the sky's space, temporarily blotting out the sun. Commuters were making their way to their respective jobs, it was a lovely day for a stroll in the park. Some people had chosen this route deliberately. Using the park to cut through to go to work, or simply walking through the park to admire the lovely flowers. They were able to soak in the early morning sunshine, which was now shining down between the clouds.

The surgeon was in the park, this was a lovely morning full of expectation and hope. Walking along the path the surgeon headed towards a large expanse of water. It was so relaxing to see the ducks floating along on the still water.

'What a lovely day this is, it can only get better.' The surgeon thought.

There was nothing the surgeon would like better than for this ordeal to be totally over. Alas, this was not going to be the case. There were still a lot of loose ends to tie off first. The last thing the surgeon wanted at this moment in time, was for the police to catch on to what was happening.

Hopefully, this would be the last hurdle before

the surgeon could finally put all this in the past, and to be able to get on with a normal life again. This was a bit of a tall order but it was not impossible.

The sun was burning down on the surgeon's exposed arms.

'This isn't very good, too much exposure to the sun can cause skin cancer. It was time to cover up. In more ways than one.'

In the beautiful sunshine, the surgeon fantasised how all those loose ends would eventually be tied up and eliminated.

'It's a shame that the nurse Gabby, would never live to tell the tale. She was an innocent necessity and although it was unfortunate, she would have to die.'

The surgeon thought.

'Then of course there was the squatter, some homeless person. Even though she didn't appear to be all there, because she had been talking to herself. She would have to be the next victim."

It had been unfortunate that the patient had rejected all the hearts, but it wasn't for the lack of trying. There was also the brother who had caused chaos to the otherwise well thought out plans, going it alone and doing his own thing. That would take some covering up, he would have to comply to the rules from now on.

'I like today, beautiful sunshine and a plan it can't be bad. I'm going to get something nice to eat, then I'll go and visit my lovely nurse. Yes, that is a good idea.' The surgeon thought.

The food was good, washed down with a glass of white wine. The surgeon felt contented, life felt good at that moment. Looking around the pub, there were a few business people having a lunch break. Dressed in their fine business suits, they were just a load of hot and bothered stuffed shirts.

The background noise consisted of chatter, laughter and soft music. Which was piped through the many speakers that were located in various corners of the pub. This had a relaxing and soothing effect, the surgeon felt that it would be very easy to just nod off.

The thoughts that were floating around inside the surgeon's head, were drifting along with the soothing noise. The surgeon fought the drowsiness of sleep as heavy eyes started to close.

'This will never do. I really must get up and take a little walk. I need to wake up and put the rest of today's plan into action.' The surgeon thought heading towards the exit.

Feeling contented and happy this was undoubtedly a good day.

The sun was still shining outside, the warmth added an extra boost to enhance the feel good factor to what was already an amazing day.

Following the path back through the park, the surgeon grinned at the thoughts of a date with a nurse called Gabby. With quickening strides, and a growing sense of excitement, the late afternoon was beckoning.

'Not long now.' The surgeon thought *'Not long now.'*

46

In her dream, she could see the old operating theatre again. The layout was the same as in the other dreams she'd had before. There wasn't anyone present, but she noticed that the surgeon had switched off the life support machine of a patient in a side ward.

Janny knew that she had experienced another premonition, but this time she felt she was heavily involved in some way. She couldn't quite put her finger on it, but instinctively knew that this could be a big break in solving the case. Janny had recognised what she thought was a place in Drayfield, two miles from Hairdale. She made a mental note to check it out.

Not wanting to go behind Chrissie's back, she would have to inform her as soon as she was sure it was the right place. There was no way she would make the same mistake she'd made in the stamp master case. That had almost cost her life.

*

Chrissie received a phone call from Janny informing her of the whereabouts of the missing person Gabby Fielding. Janny told her that the nurse had been taken to hospital. She had apparently been abducted and held captive. Chrissie thanked her and she set off with a backup squad to the hospital to interview her.

Janny was already there at the hospital, when Gabby had been admitted. She let the medics do their thing, then set to work checking her out for any traces of evidence that might be on her body or clothes. She carefully bagged up all Gabby Fielding's clothes ready for forensic testing. Then she performed a full body examination, looking for any outward signs of physical abuse and used a rape kit test. When she had completed the tests, all the collected trace, clothing and test samples were sent to the lab.

That done she rang Chrissie to inform her.

Janny had forgotten to mention the dream she'd had during the night. It would have to wait for now. Chrissie was already on her way, but Janny decided to have a quick look at the location in her dream. She was almost certain that it was the place she had suspected.

Gabby hadn't known the exact location of the building she'd been held in. Not knowing the area very well, she couldn't enlighten them. When she'd arrived at the building she had been unconscious. When she escaped she'd just kept running and not taking much notice of where she was. Going on the limited information Gabby managed to give her; Janny was almost certain that the description matched the place she had seen in her dream.

She didn't really want to involve Chrissie unnecessarily, at least not until she had verified that it was an actual location. So she'd decided to send her a text as soon as she arrived at the old disused hospital.

Janny checked that she had her mobile phone and that it was fully charged before setting off. Chrissie would send a backup team as soon as she received her message; she had no doubts about that. Chrissie was going to thank her for this later.

47

Chrissie heard the ping of her mobile phone indicating that she had received a message. Checking the caller ID, she noticed that it was from Janny.

She smiled but didn't open up the message, Chrissie would read the message later when she had more time in which to digest it, now was certainly not the time.

Chrissie was already on route to the hospital, she intended to interview Gabby Fielding. Hopefully, Gabby would be able to fill in a few of the missing blanks in her investigation.

Janny checked her mobile phone, no reply from Chrissie yet. She hoped that Chrissie had received her message. She checked the message again, it had definitely been sent. There was no read receipt, so she knew that Chrissie hadn't read it yet. Maybe she should ring her direct. She pressed the quick dial for Chrissie's number and waited for the connection. She was not answering her phone, this was interfering with her plan. Janny wanted to enter the building but didn't think she should without Chrissie being aware of it.

Janny quickly typed out a message. This would inform Chrissie where she was and enough information to direct her to the old disused hospital. That done she intended to go there to investigate the situation.

'I'll contact Chrissie as soon as I arrive there and check to see if she has picked up my messages and missed call. If not, then I'll decided whether or not it's safe to investigate the building without her back up. If in doubt I won't go inside, I'll keep trying to contact Chrissie until I get through to her. Yes that's the plan.' Janny thought.

The old hospital looked deserted, but instinctively Janny knew that this was the place. She had seen in this in her premonition dream. She recognised the building and for the first time since she had decided to investigate, Janny felt apprehensive. A cold shiver ran down her spine as she entered the old hospital's grounds. She took out her mobile phone and checked for any replies. Nothing yet, she sent another text to Chrissie.

There was a dense growth of bushes and foliage which was going to help to provide some cover for Janny's approach the old building. She stayed close to the bushes while she checked her phone one more time.

No reply.

Janny made a decision and sent one last message to Chrissie before making her move towards the disused hospital. She entered the hospital through what looked like a broken door, by the looks of it, this had already been used as an entrance to the hospital. The door was unlocked and easy to access. Stealthily and silently, she entered what was once a long hospital corridor. It felt eerie, she could sense danger here. Janny recognised it as part of her premonition dream. She felt uneasy, this may have been a bad idea.

'Come on Chrissie, acknowledge the messages please. I really need to know that you are aware of what's happening and where I am.' Janny thought.

She sent another message to Chrissie.

'Chrissie,

Please reply to my messages so that I know you are aware of what I'm doing. I'm now inside the building, I hope you pick this up soon because I'm beginning to feel apprehensive. You haven't received my calls either so I don't know what else to do. I made a decision to enter the building, but now I wish I hadn't. I think I'll get out of here now and wait outside for back up. If I'm not there when you get here it means something's happened!'

Janny xx'

The signal was getting weaker the further she went into the hospital. It looked as though the message had gone but she wasn't a hundred percent sure. Janny turned around and headed back the way she had entered. Making her way back to the entrance. She felt the need to get out as soon as possible, she felt threatened and didn't feel safe at all.

48

Chrissie left the hospital having completed the interview with Gabby Fielding. She was returning to the station, disappointed that Gabby's information wasn't what she had hoped for. This was another hot and humid day, sweat was beginning to bead on her forehead, she mopped at her brows with a tissue. Her mobile phone had been switched off while she was in the hospital. Janny hadn't been there, so she must have gone out somewhere.

Apparently the woman who had helped Gabby to escape, going on the description and the name Mary, was none other than the elusive missing patient from the acute unit Mary Smithe. So that's where she'd been hiding all along. Chrissie had asked Gabby where Mary was now.

'I don't know what happened to her. She told me to leave and get help. She said she was going back inside the building. I tried to talk her out of it, but she wanted to get her belongings out.' Gabby had told her. 'I don't know the area where I was held, so I couldn't give very accurate directions to the police. I had set off running once I'd escaped the building and didn't stop running until I felt relatively safe. I have no idea how long or how far I had run. I didn't take any notice of the direction I was running in. All I cared about at that moment, was to get the hell away from that mad bastard. I'm sorry I can't give you any more information.'

Chrissie knew that Gabby had been badly traumatised by her ordeal so she didn't push her too much. Janny had been at the hospital when Gabby was admitted. She had organised all the relevant tests and examinations, including a rape test. Gabby's clothes had been sent for testing. There had been some evidence of a forced sexual assault, but no semen had been evident or detected during the hospital examination.

At the station, Chrissie switched her phone back on. It bleeped with all the messages and calls she had received while it had been switched off.

She would check them out soon.

Sally brought her some coffee and a few biscuits, which would keep her sustained until it was time to meet up with Janny.

There was a knock on Chrissie's door.

'Come in.'

Amy Campbell entered the office, she was still a little weary of DCI Charles. As she walked in Chrissie told her to take a seat.

'How can I help you?' Chrissie asked her.

'Ma'am, I've discovered a few things while I was investigating the rape and murder cases and I thought you might be interested know what's turned up.'

'Have you documented it in a report?'

'Yes Ma'am, I have, it's all down here in this report, I thought you would be interested to know that Stewart Colt, birth name Stewart Pearce, has a brother who has heart failure and a sister who went on to become a very important heart specialist. I've managed to find out the names of the three siblings after they had been adopted. I think we now have a strong lead to the heartless murders too. This family are definitely linked to both sets of murders.'

Amy revealed the name of the heart surgeon, Chrissie gasped, and her blood ran cold.

'I must get hold of Janny, this is a major lead. Janny must be warned, this is unbelievable.' Chrissie thought.

'Thank you Amy, you've done a brilliant job. Well done.'

Amy left the full report on Chrissie's desk and left the office. She was pleased that she had gone some way to making amends for the poor start since joining the team. She hoped this would make DCI Charles give her a proper second chance, through her merit as a police officer.

DCI Chrissie Charles was panicking inside, she must contact Janny and warn her. This was not looking good. She picked up her mobile and pressed speed dial for Janny's phone. No answer...

Chrissie checked the messages that Janny had sent her and the blood drained from her body.

'Oh no, not again, please God, don't let it happen again.'
Chrissie thought.

She arranged for a team immediately, they set off at speed, with their blues and two's flashing. They headed towards the place that Janny had directed her to. The place that was mentioned in the many messages she'd sent and unfortunately Chrissie had not picked up.

49

The surgeon was angry, things were getting way out of hand. It was the surgeon's intention to return to the old hospital to kill the nurse. Then the squatter would have to be killed before finally cleaning up all traces of evidence. Anything that would reveal the identity of the people who had been there would have to be eliminated.

Nothing was going according to plan, so much for all the best laid plans and all that. When the surgeon had returned to kill the nurse, the room where she had been held captive was empty.

Stewart was also angry, his sister was on to him and the police were probably aware of his involvement in the rape and murders. He had committed the murders without his sister's knowledge. Perhaps it might have been better to have waited until his sister had sorted herself out with the transplants, but what the hell. What's done is done, it couldn't be undone, so they would have to work together to cover up their tracks.

Stewart and the surgeon soon realised that the nurse had escaped. This was the last straw as far as he was concerned. His sister should have finished her off as soon as they had failed in their last attempt at doing a heart transplant.

The final operation had failed, their brother wouldn't get the heart he so desperately needed to keep him alive. He was in the final stages of his illness, he was dying. It had forced them to switch off the life support machine that was keeping their brother alive. His last chance of survival was now over. They had been disappointed and very sad. All the time and effort they had put into saving him hadn't been enough, but at least they knew that they had done everything they possibly could to save his life. It was just unfortunate that their efforts had been fruitless.

'You are so fucking stupid.' Stewart shouted at the surgeon.

'You call me stupid? Who the hell do you think you are? You've raped and murdered three women and you didn't even bother to cover your tracks very well. You've put this whole operation in jeopardy with your actions. What were you thinking? Did you honestly think you could get away with that? So no, you have no rights what so ever to criticise my decisions. At least I was trying to save a life and not just killing for the sake of killing.'

'What do you suggest we do now, you clever shit. You think you are so bloody above everyone else because you did well in your life. You had all the opportunities, you were the lucky one. Don't you ever bloody judge me again, you should have got rid of the nurse and that head case squatter while you had the chance. It's too late now, they've escaped and it's only a matter of time before the cops come and discover what we've done. Your precious career will be over and you'll get to spend time inside, won't that be fun eh.'

'Shut up, shut up…..you're not helping.'

They had discussed a few options, none of which were very hopeful. It was all they could do now, all the preparation and effort they had put into it had all been for nothing. The surgeon was feeling very saddened by the whole situation.

50

Janny was making her way back down the long corridor of the disused hospital. She was spooked and didn't know why. It didn't help that Chrissie hadn't answered her calls and texts. She wouldn't be aware of where she was or what she was doing until she read the texts. Janny was angry with herself, she had done exactly what she said she would never do again. What the hell had she been thinking?

'Chrissie isn't going to like this, she will be furious when she finds out.' Janny thought.

Following that thought, Janny felt a sharp blow to her head. She felt nothing after that.

Stewart Colt had spotted her in the corridor and had sneaked up behind her. Then he hit her over the head with his torch. Janny collapsed to the floor, Stewart gave her a fireman's lift to the place where they had held Gabby Fielding.

Janny had been tied up with some sticking plaster, Stewart had found it in one of the cabinets. It would hold her for now, at least until they decided what to do with her.

Mary had seen what had happened to Janny and had remained hidden in a side recess in the corridor. She watched where Stewart was taking her and followed them at a safe distance. Mary was careful not to reveal herself and relied on the voices to guide her through this. She was very afraid, but she knew that she must try to help this woman.

That man was evil, he couldn't be allowed to get away with it. Mary realised that the surgeon would also be in the building somewhere. She didn't want to be taken unawares by the evil surgeon either. The voices had warned her to leave but for once she had ignored their warnings. It was important that she helped that woman to escape. The voices eventually agreed.

Mary hadn't got a plan of action so she remained hidden while she listened to her voices. They were advising her to find something, a weapon of some sort in which to defend herself with if necessary. She carefully looked around and found an old pair of rusty scissors. They would have to do for now, unless she could find something more suitable she thought. The voices agreed.

51

Chrissie had sent a quick text to Janny just in case she could pick up the message. She knew that Janny had entered the building. Her message had said she was planning on leaving it. Janny might already be outside the building waiting for back up. Chrissie hoped this is what had happened, the sooner she could reach her the better. Janny hadn't picked up her message, her phone wasn't responding. It may have been switched off, but it was highly unlikely that Janny would have switched it off. It wasn't looking good. Why on earth did Janny decide to enter before confirming that back up was on its way? Once again Janny had bloody screwed up.

'Bloody stupid fucking idiot, hadn't she learnt anything from the last time?' Chrissie thought.

Chrissie dispatched everything from paramedics to armed response teams and police teams. She put a trace on Janny's phone just in case they could locate it. She didn't think this would be needed. If Janny had done what she said she was going to do, she would be waiting for them outside the building.'

This was the last thing that Chrissie needed. Had Janny managed to get herself into hot water again? She desperately hoped Janny wasn't playing another dangerous game.

'What the fuck is wrong with you Janny Stowers. What the hell are you playing at?' Chrissie thought apprehensively.

*

Janny was slowly returning to consciousness. She was aware that she had been restrained, slowly the reality of what had happened was returning to her.

'Oh my God! What the hell is happening, what have I done?' Janny thought. 'It wasn't looking good from any angle, no, this was not good at all.'

Janny struggled to move and realised that she couldn't because she was tethered to a chair. Gradually her memory returned, she recalled being struck over the head before blacking out. As she blinked away the darkness, slowly her vision returned, along with a pounding headache.

Janny suddenly became aware of who was there in the room with her. Janny couldn't believe her own eyes.

'Katherine, what are you doing here? And why am I tied to this chair?' Janny asked sleepily.

'Janny I'm so sorry to have to do this, but you really shouldn't have come here. You shouldn't have interfered. Not now.' Dr Katherine Garfield told her.

'What's happening here? I don't understand.'

'If you hadn't interfered, I could have sorted everything out here and no one would have been any the wiser. I had a lot of loose ends to clear up, but then I could have returned to my work. I would have been able to continue my career of being one of the best heart surgeons in the country. Along with yourself of course.'

'Oh my God Katherine, you are the heartless murderer. My God, how could you. You are one of the most respected heart surgeons I know. I c-can't believe it. Not you Katherine, it can't be you.'

Katherine explained to Janny, how she had found her younger brother Alex Wilson and how she had discovered that he had a heart problem. She had felt obliged to try and help him. She was a brilliant heart surgeon after all. If she couldn't help him, well who could? So she'd been on a mission, and had intended to get her brother any help he needed. It was her job after all to provide treatment, consultations, and if necessary to operate on people with cardiac illnesses, so it shouldn't have been a problem. It turned out to be the biggest problem she had ever encountered. Alex was so ill that he needed a heart transplant immediately. Dr Katherine Garfield had been performing heart transplants for many years. So why was it she couldn't get her brother a new heart?

'So you can imagine how frustrated I was. Even though I was a heart surgeon, I couldn't help my brother. He had to go on the waiting list. His time was limited, he was deteriorating so quickly, I had to do something. I couldn't just stand by and watch him die.'

'Katherine, I feel for you I really do. But what on earth were you thinking of? You must have known that what you were doing was wrong in so many ways.'

'Deep down I didn't want to do it, but blood is thicker than water and I knew how to save him. I had to do something.'

Katherine went on to explain that as young child, she had been adopted. Her siblings had also been adopted, all of them separately, to different families.

'My older brother Stewart Colt has turned out to be a totally screwed up liability. I didn't have any choice though, I needed his help to assist me in the operations. That, in hindsight, was a bad move on my part.'

'Katherine, you really don't have to do this, you must give yourself up. Chrissie will eventually find you, then you'll have to face up to the consequences of your actions. Don't make things any worse for yourself.'

'I can't let you live, I have to kill you Janny in order to cover my tracks. And of course I also have clean up after my idiotic brother. Stewart will have to go abroad somewhere, then I can return to the job I adore and live for. I can't lose that, you must understand. I have worked so hard to reach the position I have. It has taken many years of studying and performing so many intricate operations. I have dedicated my life to this profession and now I have the knowledge and the respect of all my colleagues. I will not lose that. I can't lose it, I won't let that happen, it's all I've got.'

'Please Katherine, think about what you are doing. As one surgeon to another, you must understand how crazy this is. You can't possibly hope to get away with it. It's only a matter of time before the forensic team and the detectives put all the evidence in place. You'll be implicated through your association with your brother. The forensic tests results will be returned soon, then all the evidence will point to you and your brother. They'll know that you had a brother with a heart condition, it will all fall into place and you won't have a leg to stand on. There is no way on earth you will get away with your crimes.'

Janny glanced towards the door as Stewart Colt appeared in the entrance.

'You want me to take care of her sis?'

'Oh for God's sake, no Stewart. Don't you think you've done enough?'

'Only trying to help sis, only trying to help you out.'

'Go and clear out the operating theatre if you want to help. We've got to get rid of any evidence before we leave here.'

Stewart gave a grunt of displeasure as he left.

'Chrissie is out looking for Stewart right now. She knows that he killed the three women that were raped and murdered.'

'I'm not too worried about that. He'll leave under his real name Stewart Pearce. He has a valid passport in that name and I can help him to escape the country. Then it's up to him what he does, but he knows if he returns to England he will be arrested. It's in his own best interest to keep a low profile. Hopefully he'll heed that.'

Katherine made her way to a medical cabinet. She opened it and got out a hypodermic syringe and a vile.

'I'm going to give you a lethal injection Janny. You won't feel a thing. I'm so sorry it had to end this way, I really am. I'm sorry I have to do this, it's a waste of a brilliant talent. It's a shame, but there is no other way, I have no choice.'

'Can you smell burning?' Janny asked.

'Yes I can, so this had better be quick. I've no idea what that is. I'll have to go and investigate as soon as I've taken care of you Janny. I just hope it isn't my stupid brother up to something else that could jeopardise the situation.'

52

Mary was watching the two women from outside the doorway, keeping herself well hidden. The voices had told her to be careful, but she didn't need reminding.

A strong smell of burning was entering the corridor.

'That isn't good.' Mary thought.

The voices agreed.

She'd seen the man leave the room, so she was aware that it was only the woman she'd have to overcome. If she was to rescue the woman tied to the chair she would need to make her move soon. Mary looked around for something she could use as a weapon. The rusty old scissors she had found earlier weren't very practical as a weapon. She would need something more solid or sharper. Then she noticed a mini fire extinguisher on the floor. It had at some stage been attached to the wall. That would have been before the old hospital had closed. It was a slightly smaller version of the usual standard size, and wasn't as heavy to pick up as a full sized one. This she thought would serve her well as a weapon.

Armed with the weapon, Mary quietly positioned herself ready to spring when the opportunity arose. She watched as the surgeon was preparing to euthanize the woman that was tied to the chair with a lethal injection.

Mary knew she had to stop her before she had chance to inject the poison. She looked around outside the door to make sure no one was there. When she was sure it was clear, she rushed in through the door and struck Katherine over the head with the fire extinguisher. The dull penetrating sound of Katherine's skull being crushed in was quite sickening. She dropped to the floor with a thud and the syringe with its lethal contents shot across the floor as she fell.

Janny couldn't believe what was happening. She had resigned herself to the fact she was going to die. At first she had thought it was Chrissie arriving in the nick of time with the cavalry.

Mary grabbed a pair of scissors from the table and cut through the sticking plaster tape that was holding Janny to the chair.

'Hurry, this way.' Mary said as she led Janny towards the exit.

As they ran along the corridor Mary pointed in the direction of the exit. The corridor was filling with black smoke and the smell of burning was very strong now.

Mary left Janny at the end of the corridor which led to the exit.

'Hurry, the exit is just at the end of the corridor. Go and get help. I've got to pop back to collect my things. I'll catch you up in a little while.' Mary wheezed and coughed as she started to walk away from Janny.

'No, don't go back, there isn't time, the building is obviously on fire. We need to get out now. You can collect your things later once the fire has been put under control. Come on, we must get out now while we still can. Don't even think about going back in there, the smoke will kill you even if the fire doesn't. Come on let's go.' Janny shouted.

It was too late, Mary had already taken off in the direction they had just followed. Janny tried to shout to her, but she couldn't muster up enough breath, she was coughing and wheezing from the smoke inhalation. Mary considered lighting a cigarette, which usually helped to stop her coughing, but thought better of it in this case.

The voices agreed.

Janny's first reaction and instinct was to follow Mary back into the building. That wasn't even an option now as the black smoke found its way through the corridor filling it up with thick black toxic smoke. Reluctantly, Janny staggered toward the exit that Mary had pointed out to her. It was impossible to see now, her lungs felt like they were going to explode. She took off her lightweight jacket and wrapped it around her mouth to try and stop any more toxic smoke getting into her lungs.

Mary had managed to get as far as her makeshift digs and was collecting her few belongings and packing them into her hold all. Stewart Colt had seen her as she was returning to her digs. He sneaked up on her and stabbed her repeatedly, finally stabbing her fatally in the heart. The voices had softly comforted

Mary Blithe as she passed over to a better existence.

'Oh, look there is a lovely bright white light. Should I go there?' Mary thought as her spirit left her earthly body.

The voices guided her in the direction of the light.

'It looks lovely there, I'll make this place my new home. I'll be safe here and I won't have to return to the hospital ever again. It is so nice and peaceful here.' Mary thought as she followed the light and passed through it.

The voices agreed.

The thick black smoke was choking Stewart, he had to get out of there and quickly if he had any hope of surviving. He quickly checked the room where he had last seen his sister Katherine. She was lying on the floor and blood was seeping from the wound that Mary had inflicted when she struck her with the fire extinguisher.

Stewart checked for a heartbeat. Katherine his sister was dead. In the space of a few hours he had lost both a brother and a sister. He was beginning to choke from inhaling the dense smoke. If he stood any chance of survival, he would have to get out of there and quick. He put a surgical mask over his nose and mouth and made his way towards the exit.

53

Chrissie was panicking, Janny still wasn't answering her phone.

'Put your bloody foot down, and hurry up, for fuck's sake.' Chrissie screamed the order to the officer driving the squad car.

In the distance Chrissie noticed that black smoke was oozing out of the old hospital building. She experienced a sickening, sinking feeling deep within the pit of her stomach. The thick black smoke was rising, it increased in density as the fire started to take hold.

'Call it in, get the fire brigade, now.'

The officer sitting in the front passenger seat called in for help.
The menacing dense black smoke was billowing into the sky. It was taking on an unusual shape as it rose, it was beginning to look like an evil spirit that was being banished from the building. Like something that could be seen in the movies.

Chrissie's phone rang, it was James.

'We're almost there, we can see a lot of thick black smoke coming from the building.'

'We've called it in. Don't go inside the building. Wait until the fire brigade arrives.' Chrissie told him.

'Will do, have you heard from Janny yet?'

'No, when you get there see if you can see her in the grounds.'

'Ok, we've arrived here now. I'll get the grounds checked out. What's you ETA?'

'We'll be there in two.'

Chrissie could hear the sound of the sirens in the distance. The fire engines were approaching with the flashing blue lights and loud sirens, it wouldn't be long before they arrived. Chrissie was relieved that they were making such a rapid response. Those vital extra few seconds could make a big difference to the survival rate, if anyone was trying to get out of the burning building it might just save their lives.

The flames that were surrounding the smoke appeared to be dancing around and rising in a magical eerie waltz. The demon spirit was escorted by the flames as if it was being transported to a hell like place in a different realm. It was mesmerising.

The squad car drove along the old hospital driveway, approaching the building and its evil fiery demons. Chrissie had already jumped out of the car before it had completely stopped. She ran towards James and Mike.

'Have you found her?'

'Not yet, we've got officers checking the perimeters right now.' James informed her.

54

Janny couldn't see a hand in front of her. She knew the general direction of where the exit was. Poor Mary, she wouldn't be able to survive this smoke. Janny wished she could go back and get her out. There was no way she could go back for her. The fire had taken a firm hold, the smoke was engulfing and accelerating at a terrific rate. She knew that if she didn't reach the exit soon it would be game over.

Although Janny had faced death before, she didn't want to die anytime soon. She wasn't afraid, but she wanted to remain in the land of the living, at least for a little while longer. She wondered if she would make it to the exit before blacking out.

Janny could hear sirens in the distance.

'Oh fuck, Chrissie is going to be so pissed off with me.' She thought as she finally reached the exit.

As Janny pushed the door open, a blast of air met her. Inhaling the first breath of air was very painful and set off a coughing spasm. With each breath, her lungs expanded and deflated as they tried to inhale clean air and expel the smoke. It was very painful, her lungs were struggling and she was finding it very difficult to breathe. Dr Janny Stowers realized she would need oxygen to help her to breathe normally again. She would need immediate medical attention. The last thing she could remember thinking before she passed out was…

'I hope there is medical assistance nearby.' She thought.'

She'd barely noticed the blue flashing lights before she collapsed outside the building.

The police officer who discovered Janny lying on the ground called in for urgent medical assistance over his radio. Janny's breathing was laboured and her heart rate was erratic.

'I've found Dr Stowers, she's unconscious and in need of urgent medical attention, I think it's due to smoke inhalation. We need a medic here right now.' The officer said as he reported his find.

Chrissie ran towards where Janny had been found. Her heart sank as she saw what looked like Janny's lifeless body. She felt a lump rise in her throat which threatened to choke her as she approached.

The paramedics had just arrived and were administering oxygen and checking Janny's vital signs. They quickly moved her on to a stretcher and put her into the ambulance.

'Will she be alright?' Chrissie screamed at the paramedics.

'We need to get her away from this smoke and to hospital as soon as possible.' One of the paramedics told her.

Chrissie asked if she could go with Janny to the hospital.

'Ok, but we have to leave right now.'

'James, take over here, and keep me posted ok. I'll pick up when I can.' Chrissie shouted.

'No problem, you just concentrate on Dr Stowers.'

Chrissie jumped into the back of the ambulance and they drove off.

DI Barrow and DS Hartley stayed with the fire fighters as they continued to douse the roaring flames.

'I wonder what we'll find inside that old building.' Thought James.

Only time would tell.

The detectives watched as the firemen hosed down the flames that were engulfing the building.

55

'Oh my God, please let her be alright.' Chrissie thought as they were arriving at the hospital's Accident & Emergency department.

She watched as Janny was whisked away through some flexible double doors. Chrissie was escorted to the visitor's waiting room. A feeling of Deja vu came over her. She had been here before and been to hell and back. It brought back some terrible memories that she had fought so well to forget.

An auxiliary nurse came in with a hot cup of steaming tea. Chrissie thanked her and took a sip, she noticed that it was quite sweet. The hot brown sweet liquid calmed her down a little as she sipped it. She switched on her phone and checked her messages. There was one from James and the team, informing her that the fire had been extinguished. It was still smouldering so they would have to wait until the building had been declared safe before they could enter.

James said he would inform her as soon as they had permission to enter the building. Chrissie sent him a quick message back. She then scrolled down and found the numerous messages Janny had sent to her. There were quite a few and she hadn't picked any of them up at the time. Things would have been so different if only she had taken the time to check them.

The hospital waiting game never gets any easier. Time passes so slowly as the apprehension and fear sets in. It destroys you and eats away at you from the inside. Her stomach was churning as she sipped her sweet tea slowly.

After what seemed like a lifetime, a doctor entered the room. He explained that Janny was recovering well from a collapsed lung due to excessive smoke inhalation.

Chrissie was allowed to see her. Apparently Janny had started to recover once the lung had been re-inflated and the oxygen had aided her breathing. She was sitting up in bed when Chrissie entered the room.

'Will you please stop putting me through all this shit?' Chrissie blurted out as she walked into her room, she was relieved to see her sitting up.

She went straight over to Janny and gave her a long hard kiss on the lips.

'I'm so sorry Chrissie, I should never have gone into the building by myself.'

'No, I'm sorry Janny, I didn't pick up your messages and I should have.'

The two women hugged and tears fell from their eyes as the relief suddenly hit them both.

Janny went on to tell Chrissie what had happened.

'I couldn't go back for Mary. I felt awful, she had saved my life. I would have been murdered if she hadn't been there and rescued me.'

'I'm so glad she was there. I can't believe it was Dr Garfield who turned out to be the Heartless killer. We would have found out eventually, but it would have been too late to save you. In fact, it was Amy Campbell who found the connection between Stewart Colt and Dr Katherine Garfield. She has certainly redeemed herself and will make a dam good detective one day.' Chrissie told Janny.

Janny was examined, and given medical instructions before she was discharged, and told to take it easy for a while. Chrissie took her straight home. Janny had been instructed to keep an eye on her condition. If there was any deterioration in her breathing etc. she was to go straight back to the hospital.

'You'd better behave yourself while I'm out, or else I'll get you re-admitted back into that hospital before your feet can touch the floor. Get it? Got it? Good. That's sorted then.' Chrissie told Janny in no uncertain terms.

Chrissie left Janny with the TV remote and some magazines, she made her a quick cup of coffee before leaving.

The old hospital had survived most of the fire damage and the interior was mostly just smoke damaged. The building had miraculously remained structurally sound.

James rang Chrissie as soon as the fire officer had given them permission to enter the building. It had been a quite a while before the building had been declared safe.

'I'm on my way, get the forensic team in and I'll need the fire officer's report as soon as possible.'

DI Barrow and DI Hartley were waiting outside when DCI Chrissie Charles arrived.

'Ok, let's get this show on the road.' Chrissie told them as they entered the old hospital.

It soon became apparent that the old hospital had definitely been the surgeon's lair. There were many tale signs in there, enough to put together the bigger picture.

Chrissie had a report in front of her. It was a full description of who the Heartless killer and her siblings were. The number of bodies that had been removed from the hospital was four in total.

Chrissie was relieved that the killers had been found, but felt uneasy about how they had managed to escape conviction by being destroyed in the fire. They would never be brought to justice and never have to answer for their crimes. She cringed every time she thought about how Janny could have so easily died at the hands of Dr Garfield.

'Thank God Mary Blithe was there. It's a good job we didn't find her before or she wouldn't have been there to save the

nurse Gabby Fielding or Janny. It could have been a totally different outcome.' Chrissie thought.

*

The Heartless killer-surgeon, had turned out to be Dr Katherine Garfield a.k.a. Katherine Pearce. Her brother Alex Wilson a.k.a. Alex Pearce, had a serious heart condition. He was on the transplant waiting list but because of the lack of donors, he had to wait his turn along with many others and hope that a suitable donor would become available. Alex Wilson-Pearce had died when his life support machine had been switched off by Dr Garfield following the unsuccessful final attempt to transplant Terry Callum's heart into her brother. Katherine's other brother Stewart Colt a.k.a. Stewart Pearce was also in the building. He was the murderer and rapist of the three women found on the roadside. He had died of smoke inhalation. The missing person Mary Smithe had also died in the building. She had been stabbed. All in all it was a very bleak discovery.

Janny had recovered enough, and insisted on helping her team with the forensics and post mortems. The morgue had become a full shop once all the bodies had been delivered.

Janny had been fortunate not to have had prolonged exposure to the smoke. It hadn't been long enough to cause any lasting damage to her lungs but she would have to watch herself just the same. Sometimes smoke inhalation damage can have latent lasting effects.

Cheryl Teal had sent Chrissie a full report

following the forensic reports.

Dr Katherine Garfield had been in the care of a children's home from being eight years old. She had been adopted at the age of twelve by wealthy parents who had funded her fees to become a successful doctor and surgeon. Katherine had boarded on being a genius, she had a very good memory and was extremely good at taking and retaining information. It hadn't been easy but she had eventually found her two brothers. Her youngest brother Alex Wilson, was like Katherine very intelligent he was also bordering on genius. He had been adopted by rich and loving parents before they had passed away. Alex had been very ill and although Katherine worked in the field of medicine which was ideal in helping her brother. She soon found out that despite all her expert knowledge, she couldn't do anything to help him. Her hands were tied, she wasn't allowed to jump the queue to find him a heart. It had frustrated her so much that she had ended up taking matters into her own hands. Using her deceased parent's inheritance, the surgeon had funded her project. She had become psychotic and fixated on helping her brother. The surgeon had found donors that matched her brother, but because of the poor operating conditions, it had proved to be almost impossible to succeed. In the end she had to switch off her brother's life support.

Dr Katherine Garfield had been on her own mission, a quest she had set for herself to help her brother. The spanner in the works had turned out to be her other brother Stewart Colt, he had spent some time in prison. While he was serving his sentence he'd managed to acquire enough medical knowledge to gain him entrance into the medical profession. He had been working in the private heart hospital where his sister worked.

The only problem was, he couldn't control his sexual urges. He had raped several women before, but this time he had progressed to murdering them. He had spiralled out of control, he had become a liability for the surgeon. He was reckless, he was dangerous and he had become unhinged. Unlike his sister, Stewart hadn't been as fortunate. He had been adopted by poorer parents; they hadn't been able to fund his studying. Stewart had also inherited the genius gene, along with his sister Katherine and their brother Alex. All three of them were extremely intelligent. The downside is that they also had some psychological problems.

Katherine had found her brother Stewart and told him he could work with her at the hospital. She had explained what she was going to do in order to save their brother Alex. He had agreed to help and it had all stemmed from there.

Chrissie read the long and in depth report from Cheryl and then she filed it along with all the other reports and evidence. The heartless murder case and the rapist murder cases were now both closed. That was a huge weight lifted from Chrissie's shoulders.

Chrissie removed all the victim's photos and evidence reports from the incident board. There had been seven murders in total. A nightmare scenario had now thankfully been solved. The seven victims had all been laid to rest. Their killers were dead too. A kind of justice had been done, the killers had been caught which was the main thing.

Chrissie read the names of the victims one last time before tidying everything away.

Heartless Murders

Alan Denning – aged 19 – Medical Student.
David Blackstock – aged 27 – Teacher.
Neil Jordan – aged 30 – Electrician.
Terry Callum – aged 45 – Pharmacist.8

Rape and Murder victims.

Jane Stevens – aged 25 – Prostitute.
Tanya Colleen – aged 32 – Lap Dancer.
Pippa Downing – aged 27 – Waitress.

Chrissie stacked the information sheets and the photos and put them all into a box marked Heartless and Rape murders. Everything had been dated, catalogued and then filed in the records department, labelled as case closed. That was it. All the loose ends had been tied up and all the evidence had been gathered. All the reports had been filed, and finally the murderers had been brought to Justice. They had been convicted and sentenced posthumously. Their sentences had turned out been death by fire. They would never return to commit any further atrocities. To DCI Chrissie Charles that was a comforting thought.

56

Autumn was beginning to make itself known. The days were drawing in and the nights were getting longer. During the day the temperature wasn't too bad but at night it was turning much cooler.

Chrissie and Janny were dining in the Halfpenny pub. They had ordered some lunch and a diet coke each. It was nice to get back into some sort of normality. They were recovering well from the Heartless murders and the other murders incurred by Stewart Colt. It was nice to be in their usual surroundings, back to normal whatever that is, even the mundane side of their work.

'I've got a little surprise for you when we get home tonight. Nothing big, just a little something to make us feel good.' Chrissie told Janny.

'Oh, that sounds promising, is it sexual by any chance darling.'

'Now that would be telling.'

Over in the far corner of the pub sat Chippy Miles and Ryan Guilder, they were eating a pub lunch with a pint. Dougie Collins had joined them for a quick lunch before he had to return to work.

'Well the coppers caught the bad uns and they

didn't involve any of us. So I guess they got it right this time.' Ryan said.

'Who would have thought it would turn out to be a bloody lardy da, toffee nosed, stuck up posh doctor eh.' Chippy told them.

'And don't forget that jailbird brother of the doc's. He was on a mission of his own by the sounds of it. The dick head raped and killed those women, he had a screw loose if you ask me.' Dougie piped up.

'Yep, he was a proper bad un he was. Good riddance is what I say. One less prison cell to pay for. Got what he deserved, fucking wanker.' Ryan said.

The theme from Star Wars rang out from Dougie's mobile phone.

'The wife wants me to call for a take away on my way home tonight when I've finished work.' He told his mates as he got up to leave.

'See ya laters.' Dougie said 'Some of us have got to go to work.'

'Laters.'

'See ya pal.'

His friends replied.

Janny was excited at the thought of a surprise,

she wondered what it would be.

'Er, um, Chrissie? What would this surprise be? Because its making me feel a bit hot under the collar. You know, a bit randy. What is it?'

'Janny, if I told you it wouldn't be a surprise would it. So you'll just have to wait and see.'

'Well in that case, may I suggest that after work we dash back to yours and then I can find out what it is?'

'Janny, eat your lunch and drink your coke. Its time to go back to work.'

'Ok boss, let's get out of here, before I lose all control of myself. Anything could happen and I wouldn't be responsible for my actions. Come on my sweet, lovely Detective Chief Inspector you go and detect, and inspect while I go and cut some people up.'

'Ohhh, that sounds awful, I know it's what you do but when you say it like that, well it just sounds gruesome.'

'Sorry darling, that was very insensitive of me. I'll go and perform an operation or a post-mortem. Ok, then I'll come home with you and we can spend some special 'our time' together. How's that sound?'

'Now, that's better Janny that definitely sounds like a good plan to me.'

The two women left the pub and arranged to meet up later after work. They were both looking forward to it.

57

DS Mike Hartley had recently been promoted to detective inspector. He was celebrating his success with his girlfriend DS Sharon Trivett. They had been to a nice restaurant and had a fancy meal before returning home.

They opened a bottle of champagne when they got home. They had a glass each, then took the rest of the bottle with them as they retired to the bedroom.

They started stripping their clothes off each other; they couldn't wait to get onto the bed.

'Oh, detective inspector Hartley, please be gentle with me.' Sharon said as she took his penis in her hand.

'Detective Sergeant Trivett, you are going to have to take orders from me now. I out rank you.'

'In your dreams my darling. I am in charge in here and don't you ever forget that.'

They were on the bed in a sixty nine position. Sharon guided Mike towards the general direction of her clitoris then focused her attention on his erection.

'Where are the handcuffs? Oh never mind, it's ok, shall I use your necktie instead?' Sharon asked.

'Er, excuse me, it's supposed to be the other way round isn't it? In fifty shades of grey, it's the woman that is the submissive not the man.'

'Shut up Hartley, you are very a bad boy and you need to be taught a lesson.' Sharon told him as she tethered his hands together with his tie.

'Roll over.' He did as he was told.

Sharon slapped his bare buttocks with a feather duster.

'You are an evil woman, Sharon Trivett. What am I going to do with you?'

'Shut up Hartley and fuck me like I've never been fucked before.'

They continued to make love with a profound feeling of love and respect for each other. Mike knew that Sharon was definitely the domineering partner, and he was the submissive one in their relationship.

'Oh well, it could be a lot worse.' DI Mike Hartley thought.

*

Later that evening

Chrissie and Janny had showered and eaten earlier, they were now chilling together with a glass of wine.

'It's time for your little surprise my wonderful, supernatural superwoman. Stand up and face the unit.' Chrissie orders Janny.

'What for?'

'Never you mind my darling, just do it.'

Janny walked over to the kitchen unit.

'Ohhh, you are so forceful, now what?'

'Start twerking sweetheart, I'm bringing up the rear.'

Chrissie watched as Janny began a twerking action.

'Mmmmmmm, you've got a fabulous arse my lovely rosy cheeks.' Chrissie told her as she held on to her bottom with both hands.

Janny teased her with her sexy twerking rhythmic movement. She was singing 'You got to move it move it, you got to move it move it.'

'Ok my little sexy tight bottom, let's wriggle you out of those slinky pinky panties.' Chrissie said as she eased the panties down and off her.

'Now open your legs a little.'

Janny obliged as Chrissie slid underneath her and sat down in front of her with her back to the unit.

'Carry on twerking and let me do the rest.'

'Ohhhh my God Chrissie, fuck me.'

'That exactly what I'm trying to do here, keep on twerking and shut the fuck up.'

'Ohhhhh Chrissie, oh fuck me, fuck, fuck fuck.........oooohhhhh fuck'

Chrissie carried on regardless, Janny's twerking turned into spasms of ecstasy as the waves of orgasmic pleasure swept over Janny. She was loving this sex, and her Chrissie so much, this was why they were together this was how it always has been and how it always will be.

EPILOGUE

Chrissie and Janny had recovered well from the Heartless murders and had been deemed fit for work.

Mary Smithe had been the unsung hero in all of this, up until now. Without her intervention there would have been two more murders. Gabby Fielding the kidnapped nurse and Dr. Janny Stowers.

It had been discovered in the fire inspection, that it was a discarded cigarette that had started the fire. It was more than likely that Mary had been responsible for causing the fire.

Mary had been awarded a posthumous bravery award, but because she didn't have family or friends to claim the award on her behalf, the award went to the acute hospital where she had spent most of her time. Mary might not have been too happy about that, as she didn't like being there. The hospital gave the award a pride of place position in a locked display unit for all to see. A fine tribute to their ex patient. She will always be remembered for the actions she had taken to save the lives of Gabby and Janny. Mary Smithe had been put on this earth for a reason. She had been given a purpose to which she had fulfilled in the highest degree.

Dr Katherine Garfield and her two brothers' bodies had been removed from the building along with Mary Smithe. It was discovered that Mary had been murdered. She had been stabbed repeatedly and finally in the heart. It had been Stewart Colt that had found her when she went back for her belongings.

He had killed her before he tried to escape the burning building. He hadn't got very far before being overcome by the smoke fumes.

Gabby Fielding was going to be okay. She had recovered well and with a little help she would be fine. Katherine had been the one who had raped her using a strap on and other means of penetration.

'I had no idea Katherine was a lesbian. My gaydar must not have been working very well.' Thought Janny.

Janny had found it very difficult to come to terms with the fact that Dr Katherine Garfield had been the Heartless murderer. It didn't seem right that such a brilliant surgeon and cardiac consultant in the heart transplant field could have contrived to turn into a serial killer. Who would have thought it? If it hadn't been for her unruly brother she might have even got away with it.

Chrissie had managed to make David Marioni the police commissioner a very happy man by solving all seven murders.

DCI Chrissie Charles and Dr Janny Stowers ME, were a couple who when they were together had a life of love, sharing, laughs, tears and most of all a tolerance of each other's failings. They were only human after all, but they were understanding, caring people who would never intentionally hurt each other.

What had gone on before wasn't a true account of what they shared. That would never have happened under normal circumstances. They had talked about it and put everything into perspective. It hadn't been easy, but they had worked through it and come out of it relatively unscathed. This was certainly true love.

Janny was beginning to come to terms with her dreams, trying to work out how to recognize and define what they meant. It would have been so much better if she had been able to read the dreams in the way they had been meant. She had been unable to read the dream where she had been involved personally. She knew she was there, but thought it was as a spectator and not as a possible victim.

In future she would be hopefully be able to determine what the dreams meant and it would get easier the more she used them and interpreted them.

She was still on a learning curve and over time this would improve. This was a gift send by God, she didn't know why or how she had been chosen for this special power. It was real and hopefully it would become an asset rather than a curse eventually. She had read many reports by specialists and scientists on the subject. It had been widely accepted around the world that there was such a thing as out of body experiences. Sometimes people who had near death experiences had gained extra insight ESP. It was also reported that premonitions and other special powers had been documented following NDE's.

Sex between the two women hadn't diminished over time. In fact the sex had improved with age, just like a fine wine. All their inhibitions had faded away and a calmer approach had ensued. This didn't take away any of the pleasure, in fact it enhanced it. Sex wasn't the be all and end all, but it helped them to release some of the pressure that they had to endure during their work. They had always been adventurous in their lovemaking. It had always worked well for them. Over the years the couple had learnt how to please each other, it had become second nature to them both now.

*

The following evening.

The two women were chilling; they were enjoying each other's company. They had finished work and were in very good spirits.

'What shall we have for our evening meal tonight darling?' Janny asked.

'Each other would be a delightful feast don't you think, wouldn't you say so eh?' Chrissie replied.

'Errrm, yes, Chrissie that would be a very lovely culinary treat me thinks.'

'Well that's sorted then, get your kit off girl and let's get down and dirty.'

'Can we have a few nibbles for desert?'

'What Janny wants, Janny can have. Not forgetting a nice fine wine to go with that.'

They kissed passionately; they made love like it was their very last time. Things can change so suddenly, so they had decided to treat life as though tomorrow would never come. In a way, it never does.

Chrissie and Janny were back to their usual selves again. They were good together. They always were and always would be.

'I wonder what's in store for us now. And where do we go from here?' Chrissie asked.

'Well, we could always drive into the sunset and live happily ever after.'

'You mean like Thelma and Louise?'

'No, coz they drove off a cliff.'

'No doubt something will turn up.' Chrissie thought.

The End

ABOUT THE AUTHOR

Pamela Griffiths was born and raised in Sheffield. On September 27th 1952; she has three children, a stepson, nine grandchildren and one great granddaughter. Has a diploma in freelance journalism, a diploma in quality and systems management. Now retired from working full time for the NHS as a Development and Quality Manager. Pamela Griffiths lives in Loxley, Sheffield, South Yorkshire, England with her partner Sandy Hoffman.

Pamela was the winner of the National Great Britain poetry competition. With her poem 'The Best of British' picked from many thousands of entries in 2016

Winner of the National Local Poem competition 2011 with her poem 'Home Sweet Home in Loxley Valley' the poem was picked out as the winner from many thousands of entries. She was also included in 'Writers of the year' book 2011.

Pamela has had poems published in over seventy poetry anthologies, Poets of the year books 2011,2012,2013, 2014, 2015 2016 and has poems included on a number of CD's and in yearly diaries from 2009 onwards.

Pamela has had five of her own poetry books published by United Press Ltd. 'Expressions of Life', 'Moments in Time', 'Life is a Spiral Staircase', 'A Sheffield Lass' and 'Under a Blood Red Moon.'

Her short stories have been published in various anthologies, some in America. Poetry has always been Pamela's first love.

Some of Pamela Griffiths' books are listed by the British Library and they are also available in paperback and in kindle format on amazon.

Pamela's work has been included in the charity books:

'Telling Tales' an anthology of short stories.
'In a word: Murder' an anthology of short stories.
'Read for Animals' an anthology of stories and poems.

Pamela has donated many of her books to charity occasions and the proceeds have gone to Macmillan Nurses.

Other books by Pamela Griffiths include:

Control The Demon – A detective thriller published in 1999 by Minerva Press
Expressions of Life – Published by United Press Ltd, in 2009 a book of poems
Whispering Shadow – A short detective story published in kindle format 2010, the story was initially

included in a short story anthology Living Proof published by United Press Ltd.

Rhymes For Little Children – Published in 2011 in paperback and kindle format. A collection of rhymes for young children. Illustrated by Pamela Griffiths.

Daughters of Sappho, Rainbow Gems – published in paperback and kindle format in 2012. A collection of Lesbian poems.

Moments in Time – Published by United Press Ltd, in 2012. A collection of poems.

Fifty Shades of Gay – Published in 2012 in paperback and kindle format. A collection of poems.

Scream for Halloween – Published in paperback and kindle format 2012. A collection of short stories for Halloween.

Beyond the Cat Flap – Published in paperback and kindle format 2012. A collection of rhyming poems about cats. Featuring guest poet and author Jack Newman, who donated one of his poems.

Ho, Ho, Ho, Merry Christmas – Published in paperback and kindle format in 2012.

Ocean's Apart – Published in 2013 in paperback and kindle format co-authored with Jack Newman. A collection of poems.

Tandem Tales – Published in 2014 in paperback and kindle format, co-authored with Jack Newman. A collection of short stories.

'A Sheffield Lass' A book of poems, published in 2016

'Under a Blood Red Moon' A book of poems, published in 2016

Pamela was also published in the anthology

'Crypto & Co, The Fans Have Spoken' As a winner in a short story competition in the U.S.A.

Three of her poems were included in the book 'Tales of the Supernatural' published by Deborah Simpson in the U.S.A.

Five of her poems were included in the 'Ethereal Erotica' - Poetry Anthology Published by Deborah Simpson U.S.A.

If you would like to know more about Pamela's writing visit:

Website: www.pamelagriffiths.com

Twitter: @pamg56

Follow and 'like' her Author Fan Page on Facebook: Author Pamela Griffiths

All books are available in paperback or kindle format available from Amazon.co.uk and Amazon.com

70406340R00167

Made in the USA
Columbia, SC
07 May 2017